FOREVER PAST

FOREVER PAST

Marty Ambrose

**SEVERN
HOUSE**

First world edition published in Great Britain and the USA in 2022
by Severn House, an imprint of Canongate Books Ltd,
14 High Street, Edinburgh EH1 1TE.

Trade paperback edition first published in Great Britain and the USA in 2022
by Severn House, an imprint of Canongate Books Ltd.

severnhouse.com

British Library Cataloguing-in-Publication Data
A CIP catalogue record for this title is available from the British Library.

ISBN-13: 978-1-4483-0857-6 (cased)
ISBN-13: 978-1-4483-0883-5 (trade paper)
ISBN-13: 978-1-4483-0884-2 (e-book)

All Severn House titles are printed on acid-free paper.

Typeset by Palimpsest Book Production Ltd.,
Falkirk, Stirlingshire, Scotland.
Printed and bound in Great Britain by
TJ Books, Padstow, Cornwall.

ACKNOWLEDGMENTS

I wrote this book during the shadow of shifting world events that profoundly changed our lives; however, the people who helped me realize my dream of finishing Claire's story were constant in their support, as always. My husband and forever friend, Jim, accompanied me on research trips to Italy and became equally absorbed in the Italian haunts of the Romantic poets; we shared an adventure of a lifetime – and there's more to come. *T'amo!* Also, I extend my love and gratitude to my mom and sister, E.A., who listened to my endless talk about the Byron/Shelley circle as I wrote the manuscript. And a special thank-you to my writing buddy, Lynn Hallberg, who cheered me along every step of the way as we shared endless cups of coffee over Zoom sessions.

Additionally, I'd like to pay homage to all of the amazing nineteenth-century British literature scholars who paved the way for me to find new ways to create narratives around these amazing Romantic writers. It's exciting to see a new generation discover these complicated, brilliant literati.

On the publishing side, I am ever-grateful for the presence of my amazing agent, Nicole Resciniti, in my life, as well as the support of the lovely people at Severn House, especially my editor, Sara Porter. They push me to new heights as a writer, while always encouraging my creative vision. You are all gems!

Lastly, it's been an emotional ride to finish my trilogy about Claire Clairmont. She has become part of my life and inspired me with her audacious, brave, and fearless spirit; and I shall miss spending time in her world. I truly hope I have done justice to her legacy.

'We do not belong entirely to this world . . . my own firm conviction after years and years of reflection is that our Home is beyond the Stars, not beneath them.'

Claire Clairmont's Letter to Edward Trelawny
Florence, Italy
26 December 1870

ONE

'They say that Hope is happiness,
But genuine Love must prize the past . . .'

Byron, 'They Say That Hope Is Happiness,' 1–2

En route to Bagnacavallo, Italy
July 1873

All of my instincts told me I was moving closer to the truth, an unknown land that seemed to lurk just beyond life's next momentous turn . . . and I could not stop now. I had already risked everything at this late stage of my life, seen men killed before my eyes, journeyed across Italy from Florence to Ravenna – asked so much of those who loved me. And I refused to allow myself to doubt the purpose of my quest or dishonor the sacrifices of my dearest ones after all these perils and pitfalls. No, I would go forward and never look back.

At least I would know the whole story once and for all.

I would learn everything that had been hidden behind a veil of deception.

I, Claire Clairmont, the almost-famous member of the Byron/Shelley quartet, could not allow myself the luxury of changing course when I was on the verge of knowing whether my daughter conceived with the infamous poet, Lord Byron, had survived the typhus epidemic that supposedly took her life in 1822. Byron had been my greatest love and my most enduring torment, but I never regretted giving birth to our daughter, even when I lost her. To have my beautiful little girl, even for a short time, had been like reaching for a flower and having it bloom in my hand, only to wither away. A forever moment, so brief and poignant.

Allegrina.

The child whom I loved more than life itself.

Was it possible that she still lived?

After the revelations of the last three weeks, I now dared to hope so. In this short space of time, I had seen my safe little world in Florence turned upside down and many of my longstanding beliefs turned inside out when a British tourist, Michael Rossetti, had presented himself to me, desiring to buy my letters from Byron and Shelley. His appearance had set into motion a complex web of events that drew me into an unexpected struggle between the forces of the past and the greedy desires of the present. It brought my old friend Edward Trelawny back into my orbit and revealed the treachery of those closest to me. A tumultuous series of events that propelled me ever closer to learning the fate of my little girl.

And the odyssey was not over, as my companions knew only too well . . .

On this sultry day, our carriage rolled along the flat, narrow lane from Ravenna to the Convent of San Giovanni at Bagnacavallo where Allegra supposedly died. Fanning myself, I glanced at the familiar faces within the carriage's interior: my niece, Paula, and her little girl, Georgiana, both with delicate features and fair coloring, hiding deceptively strong-willed natures. They had come to live with me in Italy after Georgiana's father left them and, far from being a burden to me, they had brought a lively new energy into my daily existence. Love and laughter. Yes, we squabbled at times, but I cared not because I had a family again in this seventh decade of my life. Next to them sat Raphael, our one-time *domestico* in Florence, who had become our protector on this quest – and Paula's steadfast lover. With his dark hair and boldly handsome face, he could not embody more of a contrast to my niece, yet his outwardly tough appearance masked a loyal and loving nature. It gladdened my heart to watch them huddled together as Raphael read a book of fables to Georgiana in Italian.

My dear niece deserved such a man.

'Young love is quite inspiring, is it not?' the fourth adult in our band of travelers murmured with a tinge of irony in his voice – for my ears alone. I smiled inwardly. Ever the cynic, Edward Trelawny had changed little from the man I first met during the early days in Pisa, when I lived with my celebrated stepsister, Mary, and her equally acclaimed husband, Percy Bysshe Shelley – poet and visionary. All of our lives had been entwined like snarled threads from a half-finished tapestry, and their growing celebrity, even in death, made it impossible ever to fully disentangle from them. I would always be the shadow figure in their light, just out of focus but never obscured completely. Yet Trelawny had carved out his own way, not giving in to anonymity or old age. Although his hair was streaked with gray and his skin etched with deep lines, he still had the air of a daring adventurer that charmed Mary and me.

Only recently, he journeyed to Florence to reveal finally the secret he had kept from me for decades: during Byron's last days in Greece, he confessed that he had arranged for Allegra to be smuggled out of the convent for her own safety and hidden her in the Italian countryside – then made Trelawny vow to never speak of it to anyone. I was furious with both of them. A deep and burning rage. But, much as in the past, Trelawny justified his behavior and, ultimately, redeemed himself by being my champion in the face of danger and hardship. Over the course of my life, he appeared time and time again when I most needed him. When I lost Allegra. When Shelley drowned at sea near the bay of La Spezia. When I drifted, alone and friendless, around Europe, trying to recreate the magic of my youth. In my darkest hour, he would remind me that 'many love you and you owe us your love.' And I would recall the ideals that once inspired me – then carry on. I wished that I could have opened my heart to him fully, but Byron always had it, forever.

Oh, my wayward emotions.

If only I could have tamed them.

Then again, steadfastness was never one of Trelawny's qualities, and he had had three wives as well as various *amours* to prove it. He had asked me to marry him many times, but I knew better than to expect Trelawny would ever change. Nor would I.

We were destined to travel parallel paths, only intersecting for brief interludes before restlessly moving on, unlike Paula and Raphael.

'They possess a bond that is much to be admired,' I responded in a low undertone. 'I vaguely recall what it feels like to believe nothing on heaven or earth can part me from the one I love, but events always conspired to prove otherwise.'

'Perhaps that is the way you wanted it,' he quipped.

Paula glanced up, her eyes shifting between Trelawny and me. 'What are you two whispering about?'

'Nothing, except that I am relieved we have . . . recovered from the traumatic events that occurred on this trip.' I sidestepped her query smoothly. 'Though it is still hard to accept that Matteo, our landlord whom I once thought so kind, revealed himself to be a murderous villain who faked his own death, stole my priceless Cades sketch from my apartment in Florence, and followed us to Ravenna to take my Byron/Shelley letters as well. Even now, his villainy takes my breath away. He actually intended to kill us and sell all of my possessions to the highest bidder so he could regain the luxurious life that he had squandered away. *Matteo Ricci.* I had once considered him a generous benefactor, but he only pretended to be a friend while secretly plotting against us.'

It had all unfolded at Teresa Guiccioli's villa, the country home of Byron's last mistress. She had become known to me only for a few days – just long enough for me to realize how much I had misjudged her.

'And he would have succeeded if Trelawny and Lieutenant Baldini had not overpowered him,' Paula observed. 'I am not sorry Matteo fell on his own knife.'

The memory of Matteo holding a knife to Baldini's throat flashed through my mind. I shuddered. The chief of police from Florence had followed us here on a tip about my stolen artwork and almost lost his life trying to help us. A loyal and honest man in contrast to Matteo's treacherous soul. Even at the brink of death, after Trelawny wrestled over the knife with him, Matteo remained defiant. In those final moments, he had managed to gasp out that Father Gianni, my dear friend and confessor from Florence, had lied to me about his true identity and was connected somehow to a plot against Allegra.

Non è vero – I refused to believe it.

'Matteo deserved his fate,' Trelawny grated out, his words flat and steely. 'Indeed, let him rot in—'

Nudging him quickly, I gestured toward Georgiana.

'My apologies,' he acknowledged. 'I have spent too many years occupied with the art of war, and it has been a long time since I have been around young ones as my own children are long grown. Even so, I would not want even an adult offspring to hear my opinion of that blackguard.'

Raphael nodded in silent agreement.

'Matteo was a formidable enemy – and merciless,' I added. Luckily, Trelawny had learned to fight in resistance skirmishes around the world; it gave him an advantage when confronting someone like Matteo, whose criminal network respected nothing and no one, least of all the codes of battle. 'He would never have simply disappeared from our lives without attaining his goal.'

'In the end, he achieved nothing.' Trelawny gave a diffident shrug and then began to discuss the sweltering Mediterranean weather this summer, a much-needed diversion from this dreary topic.

Granted, the air *had* taken on a heavy feel over the last month, dry and hot.

The Italians had an expression for it: *un caldo brutale* – a brutal heat.

It was all of that, and more. As if on cue, the carriage bumped over a pothole in the road, and a puff of dust flew in the open window, causing all of us to cough. I held up a lace handkerchief to block my face from the gritty blasts; it provided only a slight filter.

To distract myself, I reached for the well-worn leather volume of Byron's poetry that Trelawny had set between us on the seat; he never traveled without it. As I flipped the book open, the pages seemed to part of their own volition to *The Dream*, Byron's melancholy exploration of his life – as an innocent boy, an ambitious young man, and a weary middle-aged pessimist.

> Our life is twofold: Sleep hath its own world,
> A boundary between the things misnamed
> Death and existence . . .

I snapped it shut again.

Too dreary again.

It was better to focus on the better times ahead. In spite of the discomfort of the trip, every mile was at least one step closer to the convent of San Giovanni at Bagnacavallo. When we had stopped at the convent only a few days ago, the abbess had agreed to meet with me to discuss Allegra's time there as a student. At my behest, she had checked the nunnery's records and found Allegra's name on the list of young girls who died in the typhus epidemic. She expressed her condolences and sent us on our way. But the abbess's kind overture hid a stunning omission, according to Teresa Guiccioli, whom we met shortly afterwards. The nun had been the young novice in charge of Allegra: Sister Anna.

'You have turned very thoughtful, Aunt,' Paula said quietly.

Sighing, I lowered the handkerchief. 'Do you think the abbess *deliberately* misled us, believing we would never learn the truth?'

She and Raphael both nodded.

'But why?' I exclaimed. 'She had nothing to gain—'

'Except to preserve her reputation from ill deeds of the past,' Trelawny cut in.

'It was not her fault that the convent students fell ill,' I pressed. 'Typhus was a common scourge of schools then.'

Paula's brows knitted together in a thin, questioning line. 'I cannot pretend to understand her motivation; it is hard to imagine that a nun, of all people, would have left out such an important detail.'

I turned toward Trelawny. 'What do you think?'

'The saint can lie as well as the sinner.' He stroked his beard meditatively. 'It opens up possibilities, though, about what she was not willing to reveal.'

It does indeed.

Leaning my head back against the padded silk cushion, I began to speculate about her likely sinister intents: had the abbess been in league with Byron's enemies? Did *she* wish harm on Allegra? And was she intent on making sure we learned nothing further? When I could take the speculations no longer, I closed my eyes and tried to calm my thoughts with happier visions of days gone by with family and friends. Mary. Shelley. Byron. Always with me in my heart and mind. Eventually, I began to drift into that space between reality and sweet memories – my own version of *The Dream* . . . I saw myself in Switzerland during that 'haunted summer' of 1816 as a young woman of eighteen with the saucy recklessness of one who longed for adventure, already in love with Byron, wanting so desperately for him to adore me in the same manner that Shelley idolized Mary. We sailed Lake Geneva on sparkling days when the clouds cleared; then, in the evenings, Mary and I listened as Byron and Shelley debated about poetry and science. They all penned brilliant works, and I wrote my own novel – long lost, but my best attempt at a literary jewel. We lived for love. And I was already pregnant with Alba (later named Allegra) by the time those halcyon months ended.

I saw myself at Bagni di Lucca, near Florence, a few years after I bore Allegra and had given her up – soaking in the hot waters of the *terme* with Mary and Shelley as I tried to heal from the wreckage of my life. While we sat near the warm pool, she read reviews of her brilliant novel, *Frankenstein*, and he recited passages from his poem, 'The Cloud.' I found a measure of peace again.

I saw myself with Trelawny in Pisa after Shelley drowned at sea, floundering in my grief, knowing our enchanted circle of friends had dissolved forever; it was a night of hidden desire and fading dreams, Trelawny and I desperately reaching out to each other for something solid and real to hold on to before we surrendered to being alone.

I saw myself as a governess in Russia, when I learned that Byron died in Missolonghi, Greece, weeping as the great bells of the Zagorski Monastery rang out to mark his death; time itself seemed to stop. Afterwards, Mary kept writing for me to join her in England, and I returned to nurse my mother until she passed away. Then I left England, never to return. Mary was already ill and died without my seeing her again.

And, finally, I saw myself in Florence, the city of light and shadow, living out the last of my days surrounded by the love of my niece and her daughter. It had been a full life with more to come, though what it would be, I could not say for certain . . .

Feeling a gentle shake of my shoulder, I heard Trelawny murmur, 'We have arrived.'

Instantly, my eyes opened and I beheld the Convent of San Giovanni, an ancient structure with its Baroque façade and colonnade-laden walkways across the front; it had a stark appearance with small, symmetrically spaced windows dotted along the outside walls. No trees or flowers softened its appearance. At first sight, two days ago, it had appeared severe and forbidding, but now it seemed to beckon with unexpected possibilities.

Once the carriage halted, Paula handed a sleepy Georgiana to Raphael, and upon their exit, I could not resist reaching out and brushing back one of the child's stray curls. *So like Allegra.*

Trelawny then followed, assisting us to climb down.

Once on *terra firma* again, I touched the heart-shaped locket at my throat which had been my mother's last gift to me, praying that *la bella fortuna* had followed us here. 'Paula, I would like for Trelawny and me to meet with the abbess alone. This may be a rather . . . strained discussion, and Georgiana is too young to hear such things. We can join you afterwards in the courtyard and fill you in on the details. Please, you must do this for me.'

My niece did not respond, but Raphael placed a hand on her arm and murmured a few words of agreement in Italian. She nodded. 'But I want to know *everything*,' she said pointedly at me.

'I promise.' Watching them move away, I waited until they disappeared under an archway before I commented to Trelawny, 'She is her own woman, and I cannot fault her for it. My brother, Charles, raised her to be an independent woman – God rest his soul.'

'A true Clairmont.' He smiled. 'She rather reminds me of you at that age, knowing your mind, fixed on what you wanted, and never being deterred.' He steered me toward the wooden front door and clanged the iron knocker which was fashioned in the shape of a large cross and painted in a bold red with black trim – the blood of Christ and submission to God.

Rapture and restraint.

The door suddenly swung open, and a young novice appeared to escort us through the entrance.

As we followed her, I blinked several times to adjust my eyes from the bright sun to the dim interior. As my vision cleared, I took in the white walls and bare floor – quite a contrast from the intense colors that greeted us. And it smelled like moss and flowers. Looking down the hallway, I spied the abbess striding purposefully in our direction, her long skirt fanning out in her wake like a rippling wave. As she approached, her displeasure was evident in the tense line of her mouth as she dismissed the novice.

'*Madre.*' I greeted her while Trelawny gave a brief nod.

'Signora Clairmont, I was surprised to receive a note about your intended visit so soon after the last one,' she began. 'I thought we had completed our business.'

'Not exactly,' I corrected her. 'When we left, it was on the understanding that you knew nothing more about my daughter than you had found in the convent's records. But Contessa Guiccioli told us otherwise.' I paused and studied her aging face for a reaction but saw only a slight deepening of the lines around her eyes. 'You know what happened to Allegra, do you not, *Sister Anna?*'

Turning very still, she weighed me silently for a few moments, then, finally, turned and motioned for us to follow her down the quiet corridor with only the echo of our footsteps breaking the silence – a hollow, tapping sound. As we passed somber marble statues of various saints, the abbess paced ahead, determinedly keeping her back to us – not providing a congenial history of the fourteenth-century nunnery as she did on our previous visit. *She is distraught.*

Once inside her office, a sparsely furnished room with a mahogany desk and two high-backed chairs, Trelawny and I seated ourselves. The abbess took her position behind the desk, hands folded, waiting.

While I composed myself, I took a brief glance at the painting of the Madonna and Christ-child that hung on the wall directly behind her, registering Mary's loving focus on her baby as she nestled him in the folds of her scarlet dress.

A mother's fiercely protective embrace. It gave me the impetus to begin. 'I would like to know why you did not tell us the truth on our previous visit not long ago.'

'You certainly waste no time, Signora.' Her fingers tightened visibly.

Trelawny cleared his throat deliberately. 'You not only pretended to check the convent records, which you knew only too well, but you omitted to confess the role you played during Allegra's illness, did you not?'

'*Sì.*' Her voice cracked as if the word sliced apart the reality from the lie. 'I must apologize, Signora, for not revealing that I had a connection to your daughter . . . I have no excuse, except to say I was too ashamed and guilt-ridden to reveal—'

'Whether she died or not?' I demanded.

'Please, let me explain.' The abbess held up a hand. 'I was only a seventeen-year-old novice when I was put in charge of a dozen young girls who were students here – including Allegra. I was their teacher and their caretaker. I loved them dearly as if they were my own daughters and, when typhus struck the convent, I nursed all of them, heart and soul, alongside a physician from Ravenna. But many of the students died, and no one from Bagnacavallo would bring medical supplies because they were afraid of getting typhus themselves. I sent word to Lord Byron in Pisa that his daughter was in grave danger, and he wrote to the doctor several times. Eventually, he sent his servant to collect her: a stocky, black-bearded man who carried pistols in his sash—'

'Tita Falcieri?' Trelawny queried. 'Are you certain? He was not a servant, but Byron's bodyguard.'

A man among men. Venetian gondolier and loyal guardian to Allegra.

'*Sì* – Tita,' she agreed readily. 'He bravely faced the sickroom, even though I warned him about the danger of the illness. But he insisted that we watch over Allegra together, hour after hour, trying to calm her feverish state. When I left to lead evening prayers, he still remained with her, and by the time I returned, he informed me that Allegra had . . . succumbed. Of course, I wanted to say a final prayer over her to St Joseph, but Tita would not allow me in the room again until he wrapped her in linen cloths – instructing me to place her on the list of the deceased and not to tell anyone he had been there. I complied. Who was I to question him after such a tragedy? I was desolate myself at her loss and the rest of my beloved students as well. Only one survived . . .' She broke off as a few tears trickled down her face. 'I did everything I could to save Allegra. Her passing crushed my heart.'

'Mine, too.' I choked back a sob.

'Of course,' she demurred. 'I did not intend to diminish your grief in any way, Signora, by revealing my own remorse.'

Trelawny leaned forward. 'Which girl survived the epidemic?'

'Antonia Gianelli.'

'And you never saw Allegra after she died?' he continued, placing a hand on her desk.

'No . . . Tita arranged for her to be taken away almost immediately for burial in England.'

A sliver of hope sprang up inside of me. '*Madre*, is it possible that Allegra was still alive when Tita took her away?'

She stiffened. 'You are suggesting that he lied to me in a house of God? I do not believe it, especially since Allegra was so ill—'

'And yet Signorina Gianelli recovered,' I pointed out.

'That was *miracoloso*,' the abbess stressed with firm emphasis. 'Her parents arrived around the same time as Tita and removed her to their home near Livorno for a private doctor's constant care, which was not the case for Allegra.'

'So far as we know.' Trelawny watched her as if gauging a prey's next move. 'I admit that your recollections seem credible, but Byron would not have fabricated the story of Allegra's survival to me when we were in Greece all those years ago. He was trying to redeem himself with his confession, knowing he might die during the war.'

'Signor Trelawny, did it ever occur to you that perhaps he related what he *wished* had happened?' the abbess persisted in a firm voice.

Some of the hope in my heart dimmed.

It was true. Byron had often recreated the past to suit himself, especially when consumed by guilt.

A quiet rap on the door interrupted my thoughts, followed

by the reappearance of the young novice who had greeted us. '*Madre*, we need your help in the kitchen. A large number of villagers have appeared and are asking for food, so you will have to open the second pantry.'

Nodding, the abbess slid open her desk drawer and pulled out a ring of rusty keys. 'I must attend to this matter, but I promise to answer any further questions when I return.'

After she hurried out of the office with the novice, I asked Trelawny, 'Did you know that Tita came to the convent?'

'No.' He folded his arms across his chest and settled back in his chair. 'And I'm at a loss to figure out how Tita could have traveled here secretly when he was still entangled with the aftermath of his arrest in Pisa.'

'Are you certain?'

'Completely.' He drew out each syllable of the word. 'I never told you because it did not seem important – until now. But after you left Pisa, I remained and met Byron for the first time when he joined our Shelleyan circle. Scarcely a few weeks later, an incident occurred when Byron, Shelley, Pietro, and I were riding in the countryside: an Italian sergeant named Masi came galloping through our little cavalcade and caused our horses to spook. Not surprisingly, Byron became quite angry and took off after him with Pietro and Shelley. By the time I arrived, they were shouting, and I saw Pietro strike the sergeant with his riding whip. Masi then pulled out his saber and knocked Shelley unconscious with its hilt. After that, he cursed all of us and rode off. We had to return to Pisa to attend to Shelley, but Byron fumed all evening and, eventually, sent Tita to threaten Masi late in the night. They had a scuffle, and Tita ended up being arrested.'

A vague memory stirred inside of me. 'I think Shelley did relate it to me, but I scarcely registered it at the time.'

'Not surprising since, shortly thereafter, you had to cope with the loss of Allegra.'

And everything became a total blur of chaos and confusion.

'At any rate, Tita was tried and sentenced to a short prison term in Florence, and the police cut off part of his beard to shame and humiliate him. Byron said he tried to secure his early release, but the authorities wanted to make an example of Tita by imprisoning him and then, later, sending him into exile on the northern Italian border. He was banished about the same time that Allegra fell ill, though I know nothing more of his circumstances.'

'So, Tita *could* have been with Allegra?' I posed.

'Possibly – if Byron found some way to have him secretly travel to the convent.' His eyes glazed over, as if staring off into the long-lost land of the past. 'I had left for some business in Rome after Tita's arrest, so I cannot verify whom Byron sent to attend to Allegra, and he omitted that part during our conversations in Greece.'

Rubbing my forehead in frustration, I gave a deep sigh. 'We seem to be in more of a tangle of conflicting details than before . . . Shelley told me that Allegra's remains had been conveyed to Livorno for later passage to England and, whether Tita took her away or not, the question remains: was she still alive when she was taken to Livorno? It would have been easy to hide a pale-skinned, fair-haired child among the large number of British expatriates who lived in such a large, cosmopolitan city – and pay for her keep.'

I had resided there with Shelley and Mary when we first arrived in Italy. Certainly, the Italian port held great charm with its waterside promenade and fortress on the harbor – a prettier version of Venice with its interlaced canals and irresistible to anyone wishing to avoid a British winter. But we had been too restless to stay there for very long.

'Also, it would not have been impossible to find a sympathetic Italian family willing to conceal Lord Byron's child.'

'I still have an old friend who works for a bank in Livorno; it may be worth sending him an inquiry about any funds Byron may have transferred there after we arrange to talk with Teresa again,' Trelawny commented.

'That would be helpful.' I gazed up once again at the portrait of Mary holding the naked Christ-child, her long red curls touching his arms as she lightly held his hand. He held out a blooming strawberry plant, the offer of life and redemption for humanity. *Santa Maria, Madre di Dio.* 'I wonder who painted this beautiful work? Surely, it had to be someone inspired with the Holy Spirit.'

'Probably some local artist whose name we will never know.'

'Sadly so.'

Just then the door slowly creaked open, and the abbess re-entered. Trelawny shot me a warning glance and said under his breath, 'Say nothing more about my friend in Livorno.'

The abbess positioned herself under the portrait of the Madonna, facing us with a slight air of impatience in her stance. 'I apologize for the interruption, but there are many locals in desperate need of food while trying to plant this year's harvest – and the convent turns no one away.'

'An admirable policy,' Trelawny quipped, though his tone seemed unimpressed.

She spread her hands wide, almost in supplication. 'Signora Clairmont, I know you may not want to hear this, but I really have nothing else to offer you about Allegra because I do not see how she could have survived. I am deeply sorry.'

My heart squeezed in pain. Was she right after all?

'Only Lord Byron would know for certain, of course,' she added. 'And, sadly, all we have is what he shared with Signor Trelawny.'

Since Byron chose not to tell me himself, I reflected with some bitterness.

In fact, I heard the account of Allegra's purported death almost a full week after it occurred. Shelley and Mary hid it from me for five days, supposedly to find 'a proper time,' which took place in the parlor of the Casa Magni on the Bay of La Spezia. Ironically, it had been a pleasant spring afternoon when the air from the courtyard wafted in with the scent of roses and lilacs – hardly the kind of day to expect such devastating news.

The delay did nothing to blunt my sorrow.

Pushing those unwelcome thoughts out of my mind, I came back to the present. '*Madre*, while it is unfortunate that Byron did not relate all of the details to Trelawny, your own dissembling is almost worse.'

'*Mi scuso* – I apologize.' She bowed her head briefly. 'But now that you have received what you came for, I assume that you will return to Firenze.'

'Eventually.' I rose and slipped the velvet handles of my

bag on to my wrist. 'No matter whether we return sooner or not, I will continue to seek out what happened to Allegra.'

Trelawny stood next to me.

'If I were her mother, I would probably do the same,' she conceded.

Starting to turn away, I hesitated. 'One more question: when Tita left, did he take Allegra's belongings with him? Her clothing, letters, jewelry . . .'

'No. Her clothing was distributed to the poor in Bagnacavallo, most of her letters burned, and the jewelry returned to Lord Byron, all according to his wishes.'

An acute sense of loss assailed me. *All of my letters to her were gone – reduced to ashes and dust.* I had crafted every communication with love and motherly feelings, so to burn them seemed so heartless, underscoring how I had been thoroughly eliminated from Allegra's life at the time.

'Tita was most specific on that issue,' she continued. 'The only piece of jewelry that we did not return to Lord Byron was a small pendant that Allegra wore on a gold chain – a *cornetto*. She refused to remove it when she grew ill, and it was still on her when she was . . . removed from the convent.'

The cornetto.

Only days ago, I had dreamed of Allegra wearing the horn-shaped charm around her neck. When I told Trelawny, he thought perhaps I had seen someone wearing the charm since many Italians wear them to ward off the *malocchio* – the 'evil eye.' A natural inclination for a mother to imagine her daughter wearing one. It seemed plausible because I never saw Allegra wear a *cornetto*. Yet I felt odd about the dream.

'I did not approve of the pendant since it would have been more appropriate to wear the holy cross, but she was quite attached to the piece.' The abbess's voice held a thread of disapproval. 'I wish I had some of Allegra's precious items to give you, Signora, but there is nothing left of her presence here. All I can offer you is to see her room again, if you like.'

I did not respond.

During our previous stop, I had visited the modest space where Allegra resided in her stay at the convent; it had been an emotional experience, and I felt I connected with her in a way that stretched over time and bonded me again with her memory. A forever sense of my daughter. I had even discovered where she had etched her initials, 'AB,' in the glass window near her bed. But seeing the room again so soon might stir up a fresh wave of grief – especially after this long, tiring day. I wanted to cherish what had happened in that space when I could see her in my mind's eye, watching her dance across the floor and hearing her laugh echo around the walls. Nothing else need be added.

'Your silence speaks for itself, Signora,' the abbess said.

'It would serve no purpose; I found the connection that I was looking for in her room during the last visit.' Hardly the way I would have handled it when I was young and impulsive, but I had mellowed somewhat during this trip. Pushing too hard often had the opposite result that I was seeking and that could be disappointing – or worse.

'Let me see you out.'

The abbess moved forward but Trelawny stepped between us.

'No need – we know our way to the courtyard where our companions await us.' He held out his arm to me.

'*Grazie, Madre.*' I took one last glance at the portrait of the Madonna and searched my thoughts for a brief, silent prayer that she would guide us in our journey to find out what happened to Allegra.

Ave o Maria, piena di grazia,
il Signore e con te.

I asked nothing else of the Madonna, my spiritual ally in this quest.

As we moved into the long, narrow hallway, Trelawny glanced down at me. 'Are you all right?'

'I think so – just a little off-balance.' I caught a whiff of rose-and-myrrh incense floating out of the small chapel as we passed it. Floral and spicey. 'I want to believe that the abbess is finally telling us the truth about Allegra, but . . .'

'You are far more charitable than I am, Claire. She might be in charge of a convent, but power is power, and she has no doubt wielded it with considerable resolve over the years.'

'You talk about her in such Machiavellian terms.' Was he

right to be so skeptical of the abbess's motives? Trelawny could certainly be cynical when it came to human nature, but I ascribed that to his checkered past. Yet I, too, had doubts about her honesty.

Reaching the end of the corridor, we emerged into the sun-filled courtyard with its neatly kept open space of cypress trees dotted along long, rectangular flower beds. Under a large oak, I spied Paula and Raphael sitting on an iron bench, holding hands under a rose arbor. Georgiana skipped around them, stopping periodically to twine wildflowers in my niece's hair. A picture-perfect family. I smiled at the aura of love that surrounded them with its promise of a bright future.

Paula immediately stood and pulled Raphael in our direction. 'Aunt Claire, what did you find out?'

Still smiling, I clasped her hand and squeezed it lightly. 'The abbess admitted she was in charge of Allegra when she resided at the convent . . .'

'And?' Paula squinted inquiringly in the intense sunlight.

I related the rest of the abbess's story, including the part about Tita barring her from seeing Allegra's deathbed, and her acceptance of his claim that my daughter did not survive.

Paula's face darkened. 'I was praying for better news.'

'So, where do we go from here?' Trelawny swung Georgiana up into his arms. She giggled and nestled into her familiar spot against his shoulder.

We should travel home to Florence – the adopted city of my heart. It was the sensible thing to do.

But . . . not yet.

I wanted to verify the abbess's story with Teresa – if she would agree to another meeting.

Taking a deep breath, I proposed, 'First, we have to return to our hotel in Ravenna and make certain the Cades sketch has arrived from Lieutenant Baldini; I must know it is safely stored away at our hotel.'

Ah, the beautiful, priceless Guiseppe Cades pen and ink drawing of the Egyptian obelisk in the Boboli Gardens in Florence: the site of my last meeting with Byron when we buried a lock of Allegra's hair at its base. He had hidden this artwork from me and, after his death, it was lost until Mr

Rossetti brought it to me, only later to be stolen by Matteo. But now I had it back again. 'Secondly, we need to send a note to Signora Guiccioli asking to see her again, so there is time to have one more conversation with her tomorrow before we leave; I want to know what she remembers about Tita's presence at the convent. Depending on what she says, we can then decide on our course of action.'

'Byron told me the truth when he said Allegra did not die at the convent – I know it,' Trelawny said in a firm voice. 'I think we should pursue every avenue before we simply give up.'

'Aunt, I, too, want to continue,' Paula urged. 'This is *our* undertaking, as well, and we have traveled too far to turn back now.'

Raphael nodded in agreement. 'My own parents died quite young, and if I had the chance to see them again, I would travel across all of Europe. A parent means everything to a child, no matter the age. If she is still alive, Allegra would want to know you.'

Tears welled up in my eyes. 'Then we are decided; I shall write to Teresa this afternoon.'

We will finish what we began.

By the time we arrived at our hotel in Ravenna, the Al Cappello, a converted palazzo near the Piazza del Popolo, we were all thoroughly travel-worn and tired. After affirming with the manager that the Cades sketch had been sent over and was locked in the hotel's safe, I took my leave of them, returning to my spacious bed chamber and sitting room: a quiet sanctuary in the Renaissance style, with dark wood furniture, red brocade curtains, and a ceiling of crisscrossed wooden beams and small frescoes. Richly styled comfort.

I set my bag on a small table and unfastened the top buttons on my cotton dress. Then I splashed water on my face and slid on to the settee, tilting back my head in weariness.

Just before I closed my eyes, my glance fell on Pietro's letters. That fateful day at Teresa Guiccioli's villa, when Matteo had followed us there to carry out his heinous scheme, was forever burned in my memory. *Thank God Trelawny had thwarted him.* In a gesture of gratitude afterwards, Teresa gave me her brother Pietro's letters, thinking they might contain something relevant to my quest since he had composed them when he joined Byron's expedition in 1823 to fight for Greek freedom. I was only mildly eager to read them as a record of Byron's journey to Missolonghi and his final days there, knowing the events would no doubt bring up too many sad memories. Sadly, Pietro died of typhoid fever only four years after Byron, still fighting for Greek independence. He was buried at the fortress of Diamantopoulos.

Fortunately, his letters survived and bore testament to those days.

Yellowed papers of bygone dreams.

Then a flash of light caught my eye . . . and I noticed a dagger lay atop the letters.

My head snapped up.

Where did it come from? Had Trelawny left it there?

A flicker of apprehension surged through me as I took in the lethal-looking object with its broad, tapered blade in a leather sheath. About twenty centimeters long, its richly ornamental grip was adorned by three blood-red jewels ringed in gold. Beautiful and deadly. But I did not remember seeing Trelawny carry such a knife, though he probably possessed weapons outside of my knowledge.

Gingerly, I started to touch it and the top letter slid out from under the blade. Catching the sheaf as it fluttered toward the floor, I noticed it was dated in October of 1822, when Pietro resided with Byron in Genoa.

Torn between a sense of urgency to confirm Trelawny's ownership and my own compelling curiosity about the letter, the latter won out.

Retrieving my spectacles, I began to read the page . . .

Genoa, Italy
October 1822

My dearest Teresa,
   We are finally settled in the Casa Saluzzo at Genoa, awaiting your arrival. It is an impressive port city, situated on a wide bay, busy with ships, and dotted with

a shoreline of massive marble palazzos. Very different from our quiet home near the woods of Filetto, but I think you will like the sunny lanes lined with flowering trees.

I still cannot believe the rivoluzione *to unify Italy is dead, and my fellow Carbonari rebels are scattered to the winds, though some of my old friends have found their way here to Genoa. We have not completely given up on the eternal fight for freedom because a life without a cause is hardly worth living.*

It is more like death.

We have prepared your apartment next to mine at the Casa Saluzzo. Byron felt it was safer for us to reside under his protection since the police watch us wherever we go. They know we were all deeply involved in the Carbonari rebellion and look for any sign that we might still be involved in secret schemes.

At least we have found a haven here. I marvel at Byron's palazzo located in Albaro, slightly east of the city – cavernous with at least fifty rooms, on a hilly piece of land surrounded by vineyards and olive trees. It is harvest-time, so the fields and groves are bursting with ripe fruit, and I find myself wandering along the gravel paths that snake around the vines, imagining what might have been if our revolution had been successful.

Alas, it was not meant to be.

How ironic that after the chaotic days of our Carbonari plots, the earth has simply moved on to the next season before winter sets in. Byron always said nature is disinterested in humanity's trials and tribulations; I now see that he was right. And yet the beauty of autumn has revived me in some ways.

Tita has finally joined us as well, his beard grown thick again after it was partially shaved by the Pisa police. Byron negotiated to free him from banishment, and now he is back – Il Barbone. *No one could hold Tita for long, not even the* polizia. *I am happy that we are all together once more as in Ravenna.*

But our little group is far from alone in Genoa. Mary Shelley resides at the nearby Casa Negroto; she visits often, drifting through the rooms like a ghost – a pale wraith who seems empty of her soul since her husband drowned at sea. She has her son, Percy, with her, but the only time she revives is around Byron when they talk about the summer in Geneva or the days in Pisa. Mary keeps saying that she is waiting for her father-in-law in England to send money for her and her son to join him, but Sir Timothy seems in no hurry . . . so she lingers.

Unfortunately, our band of exiles has been made even more complicated by the appearance of Leigh Hunt and his family. Leigh came to work on a literary journal with Byron, which has long lost its luster, and he brought his wife, Marianne, as well as their seven unruly children. They reside with Mary, yet frequently show up unannounced at the Casa Saluzzo, which Byron finds particularly nerve-wracking. He calls them 'blackguards.' But, like Mary, the Hunt family has no money to return to England, and so they stay on at Byron's largesse. Even worse, Hunt does nothing but create dissension with Byron and other British visitors by constantly inserting himself into every occasion. My lord has taken to letting his mastiff loose on the first floor to guard his privacy from the whole fractious family.

Genoa does not provide Byron the activities that stirred his blood in Ravenna when he was plotting revolution with us. Mostly, he seems bored and jaded; even worse, he has grown thin and limps more markedly from his club foot. Everything has turned stale . . .

But a recent event occurred which may turn things around: Captain Edward Blaquiere and Andreas Louriotis, who are part of the London Greek Committee, have just returned from Greece and are on a mission to find local support for Greece's fight against Turkish rule. I could sense immediately that Byron was excited to meet them – as was I. Their talk of liberty revived our spirits in a way that we have not felt since the Carbonari days.

Perhaps Greece might be on the verge of accomplishing

what Italy could not: to come together as a unified country, armed and ready to throw off the mantle of tyranny.

Byron and I wanted to know more.

If a new cause has arisen, we will want to be a part of it.

Your devoted brother,
Pietro

TWO

'Devotion and her daughter Love
Still bid the bursting spirit soar
To sounds that seem as from above . . .'

Byron, 'The Harp the Monarch Minstrel Swept,' 17–19

Ravenna, Italy
July 1873

S lowly, I removed my spectacles.
Reading the letter brought up visions of those sorrowful days in the aftermath of Shelley's death. More than any other person, he radiated the light that brought us together, and then became the cloud that lingered over us. Our tight circle in La Spezia scattered like falling leaves: Mary to Genoa, Trelawny to Rome, and I to Vienna, then Russia. All of us grieving in our own way. At first, my fiery temper would not allow me to feel anything beyond burning resentment, which smoldered over the decades, but, gradually, the flame died out.

At least Mary had her son, and I, my brother. Ironically, both of us were destined to make our own way in the world without the men we had loved. We learned to be happy without happiness – our lot in life.

In contrast, Trelawny moved on to a glorious adventure in Greece with Byron and Pietro.

How I envied them.

Even though Mary and I were relics of a freer age, we had no such options available to us, especially in a world that had shifted increasingly to keep women captive within the bands of respectability.

Even so, in my heart, I remained free.

How amusing that Byron's household in Genoa seemed to

be maddeningly domestic as he took on the role of generous benefactor to almost a dozen people, some of whom he did not even like. Never known for his patience, he would have labored under that burden.

Yet Byron never could resist helping the vulnerable, even if he might later regret the impulse. He knew how it felt to be mocked and shunned as a boy because of his club foot – and he often bonded quickly with those perceived as needy. I saw that side of him only once during that summer in Geneva when he encountered a very old woman, bent with arthritis, who sold roses on the steps of the Old Town; he bought every single flower and sent a servant every day afterwards to do the same. Before he left for Italy, he settled a small pension on her.

I wish I had seen such kindness after our daughter's birth, even though he had extended his love and protection to her. While I could not wholly comprehend Byron's motives or behavior, I felt certain that he would not have created a fictional narrative of Allegra's fate for Trelawny's ears alone. He *had* tried to save her life and, somehow, found a way to have Tita rescue her.

Slumping back against the settee, I fanned myself again. My travels in the past had never been easy, often riding horses in squalls of rain or going on foot through sultry evening mists, but this odyssey was taking its toll at my advanced age. I was not exactly the vigorous traveler of my youth.

Still . . .

My eye fell on the dagger once more, and I shivered in spite of the heat. Was it Trelawny's? He always wore a sword at his waist, but I had never seen him brandish a knife such as this one.

Picking up the weapon, I found it lighter than expected with its carved ivory grip and red jewels, their deep color glowing like rubies. If the stones were real, it was a valuable item for him to leave in my room where a servant could have entered and taken it. Slowly, I slid the dagger out of its leather sheath and noted the blade's sharp point; it could cut through skin easily and quickly. Shoving the knife back in its case, I set it on the table and covered it partially with the letters, not comfortable with the lethal-looking object on full display.

Then I rang for a servant to fetch Trelawny and heard his knock only minutes later. Moving to the door, I called out his name as I swung it open. He stood there with a wry twist of his mouth. 'You always could sense my presence.'

'Well, you have a tendency to pound on doors as if you were demanding entrance at the pearly gates.' I motioned him in. 'Saint Peter would probably spit in my eye.'

'Most likely.' I took my place on the settee, and he managed to maneuver his tall frame into a delicately carved armchair, upholstered in crimson silk with tiny embroidered roses and obviously designed for the fairer sex. 'I wanted to ask you about this dagger; it was lying on top of Pietro's correspondence.' I pointed at the weapon. 'Yours, perhaps?'

'No.' Trelawny stiffened slightly as he uncovered it. 'Interesting. It looks like a *cinquedea*, an Italian long dagger. I have heard about them, but never seen one before – quite magnificent.'

'A *cinquedea*?'

'It means "five fingers" – for the width of the blade.' He picked it up and placed it against his palm; it covered his large hand. 'The broadness made for a fearsome piece during its heyday in the Renaissance, almost more of a short sword, though not exactly practical in battle.'

'Why not?'

He turned the dagger over in his hands, carefully extracting the blade from its case before he held it up. 'You see, it is too short to attack from horseback because its reach is not long enough, and yet the blade is too big for a close-up fight. That kind of hand-to-hand attack calls for a thinner knife. Civilians carried *cinquedeas*, not soldiers, as a sign of their riches and power.'

Blinking rapidly, I felt my earlier misgivings surge into a primitive warning. 'Who do you think left it here, then? A servant?'

'I doubt one could afford it . . . besides, the sheath looks like Florentine leather.' He paused as he replaced it in the scabbard. 'No doubt an aristocrat sported this dagger as an open threat to his enemies – quite an effective deterrent.'

All of a sudden, I flashed back to Father Gianni's stabbing in Florence scarcely three weeks ago – his twisted, broken body at the foot of the Cosimo de' Medici statue. 'Is it possible this knife is connected with the one that killed Father Gianni?'

Trelawny carefully laid it next to Pietro's letters. 'If so, we may have another enemy who was linked to Matteo.'

I closed my eyes briefly as if trying to shut out the possibility of a new foe.

'Matteo had a network of criminals; they may still be intent on stealing from you,' he said grimly. 'They would know that he did not manage to sell the Cades sketch or obtain your Byron/Shelley letters.'

Biting my lip to keep it from trembling, I reluctantly let his words sink in. *Would it ever be over?* 'Why leave it on Pietro's letters? Unless it was to warn me *not* to act on something in them? What could they possibly contain that would be of such concern?'

'I cannot say for sure, but when Pietro and I joined Byron on his Greek expedition, there were many tense moments on the voyage to Cephalonia, then Missolonghi, and Pietro was with him the entire time while I carried secret messages to different military leaders in Greece. As I recall, the Turks put bounties on our heads and we had to travel with Suliote body-guards to protect us from assassins. We had no resources, except what Byron brought with him – and the Greek leaders were so divided. Yet we stayed.'

'He needed both of you,' I murmured. 'I now understand how much he sacrificed by supporting the Greek cause. I did not truly see it before.'

He swung his glance back to me. 'Byron did not always treat you with kindness, but I believe he had his reasons.'

'For so long, I hated him for placing Allegra in the convent, but since I discovered that he did it for her own protection, I realize that I have been unfair to his memory. It is a difficult thing to admit that I was wrong, but I have come to see that my resentment over the years had turned the sweet promise of better days ahead to bitter regret over the past.' Taking a deep breath, I continued, 'I thank you for bringing out the truth, so I would not spend the rest of my life resenting the man whom I once loved with every ounce of my being.'

His features darkened slightly. 'I should have told you sooner. My silence tormented me for many years, knowing I had the power to relieve you of such unhappiness over Allegra, but I could not do it. Byron swore me to secrecy for Allegra's sake. I am grateful that you have forgiven me.'

I managed a little smile. 'You have redeemed yourself, Edward. I appreciate it more than I can say that you made the journey from England to help me find the truth.'

'It was the least I could do.' His face cleared as the clouds of guilt dissipated. 'I only wish you had let me into your life more fully to let me . . . protect you.'

'Part of me wanted to accept your proposals, but I did not want to risk losing our friendship,' I struggled to explain. 'It was for the best all around.'

And it would have never lasted because Byron always had my heart.

The unspoken words floated through the air like a lost melody. Even though Trelawny and I had shared that one night of passion in Pisa, I knew nothing permanent could come of it. My emotions had been raw then, alone in the large, empty house along the Lung'Arno, a street along the river in the heart of the city. Our reaching out to each other filled the lonely spaces – for a short time. But I knew Trelawny would eventually come to resent the ghost of the man who stood between us, and I could never let go of his specter. 'I valued your friendship too much to treat you poorly.'

He turned silent, staring down at his polished, black leather boots. 'So you spurned my marriage offers as a *favor* to me?'

'It sounds very odd when you put it like that – but yes, that is how I felt.' The heat suddenly seemed more intense, causing me to fan myself even more vigorously. 'Besides, you always were enamored with Mary and, as I told you, I would not be the "third wheel" in a relationship ever again.' I knew that role only too well from being with Shelley and Mary for almost a decade as their 'companions,' which eventually caused her to grow jealous of my relationship with her husband; it caused a strain that never completely dissipated.

'I explained many times that I offered my hand to her only after you turned me down, and it was mostly out of a sense of guilt that I hadn't gone with Shelley that day he and his friend, John Williams, took out the sailboat.' Trelawny sighed. 'If I had been with them, I would have made certain that they returned to shore when the storm kicked up, and they would have survived the day.'

'You cannot blame yourself for his death . . . Shelley knew enough about sailing to know that a storm in the bay at La Spezia could be treacherous.' I reached out and touched his hand. 'Let us not open that window of self-reproach again, Edward. It truly serves no purpose, except to fill our days with "what-ifs" when no one can really know how life would have turned out had we taken a different path. If we had married, we might have ended up despising each other.'

'I doubt it.'

An awkward silence descended on the room, almost as heavy as the sweltering afternoon heat. Perhaps he was right, but dealing with our shared history would have to wait since a new peril seemed to be rising around us. 'Perhaps we should reconsider whether to meet with Teresa or not. I have not sent the note to her yet, but if you think there is a new danger on the horizon, I am willing to delay the request. Traveling to her villa through the woods of Filetto could be perilous since it is such an isolated road.'

Trelawny's jaw set in a stubborn line, obviously not quite ready to give up discussing missed chances of days gone by, but, eventually, he relented with a shrug. 'Nothing seems certain about the *cinquedea* at this point, so I see no reason to alter our plans. Besides, Raphael and I can handle anything that might occur on the journey.'

'Then I shall write to her this very minute.' I went over to the desk and jotted down a few lines. I sealed and addressed it, then handed it to Trelawny. 'Will you have it delivered for me?'

'Of course.' He took the note and pretended to study it. 'I may dine in this evening – it was a long day.'

'I shall do the same.' I tried not to notice the wistful note in his tone. 'And I suspect that Paula and Raphael might enjoy a dinner together without our company.'

He laughed shortly as he slipped the message inside his jacket. 'Yes, our young lovers should have some time alone. We can share this latest development with them tomorrow. In the meantime, I shall inquire of the hotel manager whether anyone was noticed lurking nearby, or had access to your room, aside from a servant.'

'Thank you, Edward.'

Lifting my hand, he kissed it with a tender caress and then let himself out without another word.

I touched my hand, still feeling the imprint of his lips on my skin.

If only . . .

Love and betrayal – how they drove us to the dark places from where we could not return, much as we wanted to. The depths. I knew those powerful emotions all too well and could easily imagine the dark forces that might be dancing around us, just waiting to strike.

Uneasily, I moved toward the window and watched the twilight begin to descend on the street below.

Dusky shades were creeping in again like tendrils from a vine into the open spaces.

We would need to tread carefully – and pray.

E prega Dio – *pray to God.*

After a restless night, I rose at dawn, donned a light green cotton dress, completed my toilette, and waited to hear back from Teresa. But my room seemed more like a cage as I paced nervously around the sitting area, avoiding Pietro's letters. I could not settle myself enough to read them. Instead, scenes from the last two weeks kept flashing through my mind: Father Gianni's murder, the tense days traveling to Ravenna and the death of Matteo with his final gasps of blood and betrayal. All of the images swirled together into one shifting blur of fear and uncertainty. And now this new danger had presented itself.

I had to do something . . .

Moving to the desk, I wrote a brief letter to Lieutenant Baldini and rang for a servant to deliver the message:

Please meet me at the Battistero Neoniano around ten
o'clock; the Cades drawing has arrived safely, but another
urgent matter has arisen. It is imperative that I see you.

> Yours truly,
> Claire Clairmont

Shortly, a young Italian woman appeared at my door and I
instructed her to take the letter to the police station, then ask
the manager to arrange for my escort to the baptistery. She
curtsied and left. I debated for a few moments whether to
inform Trelawny of my intentions, but I knew he would probably try to dissuade me and I could not remain confined in
my room any longer.

Baldini needed to know about the *cinquedea*.

After mulling over how to transport the dagger, I finally
decided to wrap it in my muslin shawl and headed down the
stairs, my steps light and rapid. I was probably behaving too
impulsively, but it was preferable to the unbearable anxiety
of inaction. When I arrived in the lobby, a young man who
was probably not even twenty years of age waited for me.
He gave a small bow.

'*Buongiorno, Signora. Mi chiamo Mario.*' He offered to
carry my shawl as we emerged from the hotel.

'*No, grazie.*' Smiling, I took his arm and glanced up at a
thin layer of high, gray clouds stretching across the sky like
a downy blanket, providing enough shade to keep the air
relatively cool. I pointed at the Via Cavour, inquiring if we
could take that route to the baptistery. Mario nodded and
we began our stroll down the semi-deserted cobblestone
street. Too early for socializing or morning visits, only
produce vendors appeared along the avenue, setting up their
displays of fruit and vegetables framed by bouquets of
girasoli – the vibrant sunflowers that seemed to grow everywhere in Italy.

The symbol of joy and rebirth.

Ambling along the narrow, winding street, we chatted about
the local Byzantine mosaics, and I found myself relaxing in
Mario's company, forgetting briefly about the lethal object I
carried. In the midst of discussing the Justinian Mosaic of

Basilica San Vitale, I slowed my steps, and Mario asked, '*Sta bene?*'

I assured him I was fine – just distracted by the building to our left.

41 Via Cavour.

The Palazzo Guiccioli.

In truth, I had wanted to take this route so I could pass by the palazzo once more – the place where Byron lived during the height of his activities with the Carbonari. The three-storied, rough brown structure with its green shuttered windows and massive front door once belonged to Teresa's husband, Count Guiccioli, who allowed Byron to live on the third floor. Now a quiet spot on a pedestrian street, the palazzo had once been the center of revolutionary activities – plotting, gunrunning, even murder.

'Ah, you must know the famous English poet who lived here – Lord Byron.' Mario stared up at the building's slightly crooked roof and chipped paint. 'No one resides here now because they say the palazzo is haunted by the specter of a soldier who died inside; his ghost supposedly roams the empty passageways, weeping for his lost life.'

Oh, yes.

Luigi del Pinto – the Austrian officer who had been assassinated in the very spot where we now stood.

I knew all about his death from reading Byron's secret Ravenna memoir which Trelawny had given to me. The young man had been shot by the Carbonari, though he did not die until the next morning when Byron's doctor could do nothing to save him. His had been one of the first deaths during those rebellious days and, afterwards, Byron became passionately committed to the cause of Italian freedom, hiding rifles in the cellar next to his favorite wines and commanding his own *turba* – a small unit of fighters. Sadly, the *Risorgimento* failed but, in Byron's own words, it changed him from a poet who wrote about battles to a man ready for battle.

It prepared him for Greece.

'You are quiet, Signora,' Mario observed as he peered inside one of the lower windows. 'Did you know the English lord?'

How could I tell someone so young that I had not only

known him but loved him passionately, body and soul? A woman of my age? 'It was long ago, but I was . . . acquainted with him.'

Something in my voice caused Mario to turn his head and fasten his glance on me with a quizzical expression. 'Perhaps the ghost that haunts the palazzo is not the Austrian soldier, but Lord Byron himself.'

'His legacy has certainly cast a long shadow.' *For many of us.*

'I think there is more to this story than you are telling me.'

Taking his arm once more, I continued, 'I shall count on your discretion not to relate this stop with anyone.'

He placed a hand over his heart. 'You have my word of honor.'

As we began to move on, I took one last look at the palazzo over my shoulder and imagined the scene that Byron recounted in his memoir of the day Allegra arrived. I had been happy when Shelley told me that Byron decided to bring her to Ravenna to live with him but infuriated because he would not let me visit her; instead, Teresa took my place as her *mammina*. It had crushed me at the time. But now, knowing how much both of them loved Allegra, I could gladly envision Byron standing on the front steps when her carriage pulled up. I saw him stretch out his arms to our daughter and then hug her tightly. I heard her girlish laughter in delight at being reunited with her beloved papa. A cherished moment.

Then the vision dissolved as quickly as it had appeared.

I sighed and turned away, resuming our idle chatter as we covered the short distance to the baptistery.

Once we arrived, I glanced around for Lieutenant Baldini, but he was nowhere to be seen. I was early – for once. Taking a seat on a nearby iron bench, I kept the hidden dagger close and informed Mario that I would not be too long. He nodded, then drifted off toward a small *ristorante* across the street with a smattering of linen-covered tables outside.

While I waited, I took stock of the *battistero*, with its eight-sided walls, symbolizing the seven days of the week, along with the Day of the Resurrection and Eternal Life. In shape, it resembled the one in Florence, which I had visited many times, but the similarity ended there. The Florentine structure was covered in white-and-green marble trim with magnificent doors decorated with bronze and gold panels; this *battistero* possessed none of that elegant facade. Made of plain brown brick, with small arched windows, it had little ornamentation.

'So, what do you think of the *battistero?*' A man's familiar voice intruded on my thoughts.

Rising slowly, I beheld Lieutenant Baldini, the Florentine policeman who had become our protector; he appeared to have recovered fully from his tussle with Matteo. His normally serious face seemed relaxed in boyish warmth as he shook hands with me – probably because my landlord no longer presented a danger to any of us.

'I was going to stop by your hotel before I left today to make certain the Cades sketch arrived safely, so I was happy to receive your note that it had, and you wanted to meet with me,' he said, taking in the plain structure in front of us with a slight frown. 'We can only hope the interior makes up for whatever is missing on the outside.' He motioned me to go ahead of him, and I proceeded through the open wooden door, noting how the left side had been worn down from the many hands that had pushed it open over the centuries.

Once we had entered the domed structure, I savored the cool air within its thick walls, adorned with paintings of religious scenes from the Old Testament. Nothing remarkable, until I looked up at the stunning blue-and-gold ceiling mosaic of John the Baptist baptizing Jesus in the Jordan River, ringed by the apostles.

Baldini followed my gaze, regarding the ceiling silently for a few moments. 'I am surprised at the beauty – quite unexpected.'

'Indeed . . . and, luckily, it provides some privacy away from the hotel.' After scanning the room quickly to make certain we were completely alone, I slowly unraveled the shawl from around the dagger.

As the weapon became visible, Baldini exclaimed with a touch of awe in his voice, '*Il cinquedea.*'

I passed it to him.

Almost with reverence, he handled the object as if it were a holy artifact. 'Where did you find one of these daggers? They are quite rare, and valuable.'

'It appeared in my room yesterday after our return from Bagnacavallo; I found it on top of Pietro Gamba's letters, which I had left on my tea table. Trelawny does not own it, so we have no idea how it ended up there. Do you think it was left as a warning?'

'*Forse* – maybe,' he murmured absently, his entire focus on the knife as he grasped the hilt, flexing his fingers around it. Then he unsheathed the knife and traced his fingers along the blade. 'Such beautiful, intricate etchings . . . whoever made this *cinquedea* used it as a canvas for his artistry – a Raphael of weaponry.'

I gritted my teeth impatiently.

Never would I understand the male attraction to weapons. 'Trelawny said Renaissance men carried this type of dagger to show their status.'

'*Sì*. It was part of the fashion of the day to wear it – for those wealthy enough to own one, but it also served as protection if an assassin tried to attack in the narrow streets of Florence; it could be used for a single, lethal stroke.' He placed it behind his back, holding it horizontally. 'Men wore it here, so the beauty of the hilt would be visible, but also for quick access.'

I watched him flick it with a flourish as if confronting an enemy and asked, 'Who would possess something so valuable? I can think only of Matteo, but he is dead. Do you think it might have been one of his criminal accomplices who has followed us here?'

'If so, I would think it odd for a thief not to steal your letters and other precious belongings and, at the same time, leave you a treasured *cinquedea*. It does not make sense. Then again, his plan might be more complex than we realize.' He carefully lowered the dagger. 'Another thought just occurred to me, one that you might not like to hear: you may have another enemy, one whom you know and trust . . . a close family member or friend.'

My mind faltered at the suggestion that a person dear to

me could be responsible. 'I cannot even think in that direction since it implicates Paula, Raphael, or Trelawny. They are devoted to me and have risked so much to come along on this journey. Of course, it is always possible that little Georgiana might be responsible. She is five years old and could be deceiving all of us.' A sarcastic note crept into my tone.

'Signora, I do not mean to upset you, but it had to be said.' He fastened a clear, direct glance on me. 'If you had to choose one member of your circle who might have some hidden motivation, who would it be?'

'I . . . I do not know.' My sense of security faltered. After Matteo's demise, I felt the dangers which had come into my life over these past few weeks were finally over, but I realized that I may have been premature in my assessment.

Baldini heaved a deep sigh. 'In my line of work, I have seen treachery split families apart over money and power – so tragic. Betrayals. Hatred. Revenge. It goes too far for matters to ever be resolved amicably. After all, we are the country of the Borgias where deception and death touched every person connected with them. Sadly, this type of behavior is all too common, and not only among the wealthy.'

For a long moment, I stared off into a space where I could simply blank my mind and refuse to accept the possibility of such disloyalty, but I had been wrong so many times in my life about whom I could trust. For so long, I believed that Byron had treated me ill, but I came to learn only recently how he had been trying to protect Allegra and me. I considered Trelawny my dearest friend, yet he admitted that he had lied to me for years. Could I truly see beneath the surface of anyone's behavior? 'My hunt for Allegra is far from over, though I have regained the Cades sketch. And if the knife is a warning to abandon my quest then the intruder, whether familiar to me or not, would seem to want me to return to Florence. But why?'

'Perhaps to make sure you sell the sketch quickly once you arrive, and then somehow lay claim to the proceeds through some nefarious means.'

'But I would gladly share the money with Paula and Georgiana,' I pointed out. 'No, I would prefer to believe there is some assailant, as yet unknown to us, even though the thought is disturbing. Truly, none of my companions would ever betray me.'

That was a certainty, wasn't it?

'Signora, you are a woman of resolve.' He regarded me thoughtfully for a few moments, then added, 'And courage.'

'I will take that as a compliment, even if some might call it "extreme stubbornness" or "foolhardiness."' I smiled.

'If you will permit me to keep the dagger, I shall speak to the local police in Ravenna about it and then make inquiries when I return to Firenze. A weapon this ornate, with a Florentine leather case, could have been a family heirloom, which some well-connected member of our city recognizes, so I might be able to discover the identity of its owner.' He raised his eyes to the mosaic once more, as if for divine assistance. 'I hope, by the time you make your way back to Florence, I will have some information for you.'

'I am very grateful for your help.' I crossed myself in respect of the holy images that surrounded us. 'We are hoping to see Teresa Guiccioli at her villa this afternoon, and afterwards we shall decide on our next step. Trelawny and I both felt she might have some piece of information about Allegra's fate that she did not remember during our previous chaotic visit. If not, there really is no other option than to return to Florence. At least our lives will no longer be impoverished – thanks to you.'

He inclined his head. 'I am glad that I could play some part in restoring your possession to its rightful owner, though it is a shame that you have to sell it.'

'I am happy to do so if it means Paula and Georgiana have a comfortable life.'

'*Va bene.*'

He escorted me outside where Mario was sitting on the front steps, absently twirling a pink rose. Dropping the flower, he immediately stood and took the shawl from me, placing it carefully around my shoulders.

'I leave you in good hands, then.' Baldini started to back away. '*Addio, Signora.*'

'Thank you again, Lieutenant.' I reached out to shake hands. 'I look forward to seeing you in Florence.'

As Baldini disappeared down the street, I noticed Mario was wiping his brow under the blazing sun. Now that the skies had cleared, it had grown quite warm.

'*Mi perdoni*, Mario. I would not have kept you waiting so long if I had known how hot it was outside,' I hastened to apologize.

'I am used to it. But I did not know you were meeting Lieutenant Baldini.' He said the police officer's name in slow admiration. 'His reputation has spread quickly through Ravenna. It is said he tracked a vicious murderer here from Florence and, on his own, fought him to the death. That feat took great bravery – he will be talked about for years as a true warrior.'

Hardly single-handedly. But I bit my lip to restrain myself from blurting out the truth about Baldini's role in Matteo's death. Young men needed someone to admire, and Baldini had certainly earned enough respect from me to allow the rest of the details to remain unspoken.

'Signora, is there any other place you wish to see?' Mario queried.

'No, I am ready to return to the hotel, but shall we take a different route? I believe there are some shops along the Via Gamba and I would like to find a small gift for my great-niece.' Truthfully, I did not wish to pass by the Palazzo Guiccioli again; no need to resurrect those memories. I had seen enough.

He steered me toward the Via Gamba, where I could make out several storefronts, now bustling with young mothers, children in hand, and well-dressed men carrying leather bags. I moved more slowly along the congested street, mulling over my conversation with Baldini. His suggestion that someone close to me might have placed the dagger in my room had sown seeds of doubt. Certainly, neither Paula nor Raphael had shown me anything but support and love. Even if Trelawny had hidden information from me in the past, he had redeemed himself over these last days, staying by my side through even the most dire events.

Who could be the unknown enemy?

I had no answer – only more questions.

'This is Gaetano's.' Mario's voice brought me back to the

present. 'He is a *giocattolaio* who creates wooden toys for the local children.'

I scanned the window display and saw everything from rocking horses to dolls, all made of exquisitely carved wood. After taking them in one by one, I spied a simple cup and ball which would be a perfect plaything to keep Georgiana occupied during the carriage ride to Teresa's villa. I pointed at it with a nod. Mario then ushered me inside. A tiny bell rang as the door opened and closed, which did not distract the bespectacled old man who sat behind a carver's desk, bent over his latest project: a small wagon. Wood shavings fluttered around him as he made deep cuts with a hammer and chisel, then wiped the toy with a cloth.

As I glanced around the shop, the smoky scent of cedar wafted over from the assortment of toys positioned on the floor-to-ceiling shelves behind him. Animals, dolls, and ornaments made from different colored woods, all polished to a smooth sheen, crowded every space. The fine work of a craftsman.

After Mario greeted the carver in Italian, he slowly looked up. His face seemed as deeply etched as the pieces he made, with harsh lines that radiated down his cheeks.

When I asked in Italian about purchasing the toy in the window, he set down the hammer and chisel.

'*Ho qualcosa di meglio.*' Rising slowly to obtain something better, he then disappeared behind a white silk curtain embroidered with a triangular pattern of a compass in the back of the store. A few minutes later, he returned with a similar cup and ball, but this one with more ornate carvings around the handle and a pink flower painted on the cup.

'*Ah, bella,*' I said as I took it from him. '*Quanto?*'

Gaetano stated the price in *lire*, which seemed quite inexpensive considering the hours it must have taken to create it. But when I asked a second time, he repeated the same amount with a ring of finality. After I paid him, he placed the toy in a small gift box and carefully wrapped it with a silk ribbon. Smiling, he gave it to me with a flourish of his hand.

'*Grazie, Signor.*' I tucked it under my arm.

As we emerged on to the street again, I took a last glance

at his beautiful wooden creations, and saw the toymaker was still staring at me with a pensive expression. Almost as if he was trying to grasp something that eluded him. A lost recollection. I turned away, puzzled by his regard, and Mario and I resumed our stroll.

But the incident stayed with me until we arrived at the Al Cappello. I thanked Mario for his service and he strode off, whistling an Italian tarantella tune under his breath. I stood there for a little while, listening as his retreating figure disappeared around the corner. He had the bounce of youth in his step – what a contrast with the grizzled air of the toymaker who had seen decades of conflict and wars in Italy. The fullness of life had brought the challenges of age.

'Where have you been?' Trelawny suddenly appeared at my side, his eyes snapping with anger. 'After all that has occurred, I have been frantic that you met with some misfortune.'

'I am fine,' I said calmly. 'If you must know, I went to meet Lieutenant Baldini at the baptistery to tell him about the *cinquedea*—'

'While you were out, there was an incident with Paula.'

Panic flooded through me as I clutched his arm. 'Has she been harmed? Is she—'

'Not here.' He grasped my arm as we rushed inside and up the stairs. All the while, I plied him with questions about Paula that he refused to answer. When we reached the third floor, we hurried toward her room. The door stood cracked open, and I found her standing in the middle of a chaotic wreckage of torn clothing and broken knick-knacks strewn across the floor, along with overturned furniture.

Paula looked up, tears streaming down her cheeks.

I flung my arms around her. 'Oh, my dear, I am so sorry. What happened?'

'I do not know, Aunt,' she said, her voice muffled against my shoulder. 'I went out for a morning stroll with Raphael and Georgiana; when we returned, I found . . . the door ajar. Someone must have broken in while we were gone and done this horrible thing. Most of my dresses are shredded, but nothing was taken.'

I stared over her head into Trelawny's eyes and did not like the expression I found there.

Paula finally pulled back and I brushed back the stray hairs that had matted across her forehead as I asked, 'Where is Georgiana?'

'Raphael took her downstairs before she could enter the room and was going to talk with the hotel manager.' She wiped away the tears, her shoulders quaking. 'I must compose myself before she returns.'

'Please, sit down.' Trelawny gently led her to a chair, then poured a glass of water from the decanter on the bedside table. 'Just drink it slowly and try to steady your nerves.'

As I observed his handing the drink to Paula, I was never more grateful to have Trelawny here; he could always be trusted to deal with an emergency – always calm and dependable.

We needed him more than ever in the face of this frightening attack.

The *cinquedea* and now the vandalism of Paula's clothes.

We were definitely being targeted, and the perpetrator was growing increasingly bold.

I faced the possibility that the events of the last three weeks had not ended this nightmare . . . it may only just be nearing its climax.

Convent of San Giovanni, Bagnacavallo, Italy
June 1821

Allegra's story . . .

I have been at the convent for months and months.

It seems as if Papa has forgotten about me. He never writes nor has he visited me, even though I beg him to come. *Mammina* has also ignored my letters. The nuns have been gentle and friendly, especially Sister Anna, but they did not make up for not having my *famigila*. My family. I missed them so much. When we were together in Ravenna, *Mammina* gave me toys and Papa read poetry to me after dinner in his study.

Now my days were spent with only school lessons and prayers.

I tried not to despair . . .

Many times I sat in the courtyard, playing in the shade of the cypress trees. All around me roses bloomed in clusters of yellow and pink that smelled honey-sweet. But in spite of the warmth and beauty, it felt so desolate. The days passed slowly, and I made few friends. The only girl who spoke much to me was Antonia. She was kind, but the other Italian girls whispered about me. I would hear them say *poeta scandaloso*, and I knew they were gossiping about Papa. Lord Byron – the scandalous poet. Then they would look at me with pitying eyes because he never came to see me.

What had I done to so displease him?

Last week, I asked the nuns to help me write another note to Papa, hoping it would remind him of my love:

> My dear Papa,
> It being fair-time, I should like so much a visit from my papa as I have many wishes to satisfy. Will you come to please your Allegrina who loves you so?
> T'amo,
> Allegrina

Still, he has not responded. No letters to show he even remembered that I existed. I have been crying for days.

I wanted to go home to Ravenna.

But I did not think Papa would send for me any time soon. Maybe not ever.

My whole world seemed to be confined within these walls, and Sister Anna watched me all the time – especially after that man appeared in my room two weeks ago. I had been sleeping, so I did not know what happened, but I heard the nuns speaking about it the next day as they left the chapel. Hiding behind a statue, I had listened carefully.

They said that when the old abbess made her usual rounds, she spied a dim figure in the hallway who darted into my room. She ran in and called out for help when she found the man standing over my bed. Startled, he shoved her out of the way and escaped before anyone else could arrive. That is when I awakened, puzzled to see the abbess anxiously staring down at me. After that, an old man always sat outside my room at night, and I was not permitted to leave the grounds. I told Sister Anna that I would be safer with my papa in Ravenna, but she just shook her head.

And so my life grew narrower.

I touched the little *cornetto* charm that hung on a chain around my neck, and I thought of Tita who had given it to me. Papa's bodyguard, with his wild black beard and plumed hat. He was never without his pistols tucked into his sash or a little *fritole* snack for me. How I missed his booming voice and the loving way he would sweep me up in his arms, then carry me around on his shoulder.

I would be safe with Papa because Tita was never far away, but no one would listen to me.

Sighing, I picked one of the roses in the courtyard and began plucking at its petals. I noticed Antonia approaching.

'*Buongiorno, Allegrina*,' she said, twirling around in circles, her silk skirt billowing out. 'We are going into Bagnacavallo for the fair today. There will be a parade through the town and a feast to honor the saints. It will be such fun.' She held out her hand. 'Come along. Everyone else has already left.'

Tossing the rose aside, I eagerly took her hand. 'We must be quick to avoid Sister Anna, though. She will try to stop me.'

Peeping around the deserted courtyard, she pointed at one of the brick walls. 'There is a door just beyond that archway that Sister Anna leaves unlocked on the day of the fair, so we can slip out before she knows we are gone.'

'Oh, yes.' We skipped down a narrow path, then ducked under one of the arches that hid a small door, partially shaded by a tree limb. It took both of us to pull it open, but we did it. Then I could see the street outside, filled with families who were laughing and talking as they ambled by. Everyone seemed so happy, basking in the sunlight. I envied them.

Antonia slipped out and waved me to follow her, but I felt someone seize my arm in a firm grasp.

'*Allegrina*, you know better than to try to sneak out,' Sister Anna hissed at me.

'But the other girls—'

'They are not *you*,' she said, pulling me back toward the door. I struggled, watching Antonia fade into the crowd, but Sister Anna's strength won out. Once we were inside the courtyard again, she locked the door and pocketed the key.

Feeling tears stinging my eyes, I sank down on a bench and hung my head. It was so unfair.

As I wept, Sister Anna knelt in front of me. Tipping up my chin, she dabbed at my cheeks with her handkerchief. '*Mi dispiace, Allegrina*,' she apologized softly. 'I wish I could let you go to the fair, but the abbess has given strict orders that you are not to leave the convent grounds.'

'But why?'

She brushed back my hair with a soft touch. 'I cannot say, but you must never do that again. Promise?'

I did not answer, so she repeated the question.

Finally, I crossed my heart. '*Lo prometto.*'

Hugging me tightly, Sister Anna whispered a few words of consolation in Italian, but I closed my ears to her.

I only wanted to leave and return to my papa.

THREE

'Sun of the Sleepless! melancholy star!
Whose tearful beam glows tremulously far,
That show'st the darkness thou canst not dispel . . .'

Byron, 'Sun of the Sleepless,' 1–3

Ravenna, Italy
July 1873

As Paula clutched the water glass with both hands, she took in shallow, ragged breaths. 'What do you make of all of this, Aunt?'

'Trelawny and I think we may have a new foe who has suddenly appeared.' Watching her features tighten with a mixture of fear and surprise, I felt a twinge of guilt. *This is my fault for involving her in such a debacle.* I edged around the shredded clothing and seated myself across from her, grasping her hand in reassurance. Her fingers felt cold in spite of the heat. 'He wants to frighten us with these acts—'

'And he has succeeded. I almost fainted when I saw all of my dresses ripped apart and strewn on the floor. Who would do such a thing? It is so cruel.' She lowered the glass to her lap, her hands shaking with a small tremor. 'When I called out for Trelawny and he could not find you, I was frantic, imagining all kinds of things. I am so relieved that you are unharmed.'

I heard Trelawny clear his throat in reproach, and my guilt deepened. I should have told him where I had gone, but my impatience to learn more about the *cinquedea* had caused me to behave impulsively yet again. Would I ever learn? 'I must apologize to both of you; it was most thoughtless to simply disappear like that. I met Lieutenant Baldini at the baptistery to bid him farewell before he left for Florence.'

'You are not at fault. How could you know that my room would be ransacked?' Paula settled into the chair, her shoulders relaxing slightly. 'Should we let him know about this break-in?'

'I believe it is too late; he has already departed for Florence,' I informed her.

'Then I suppose we must inform the local police . . .' Her voice trailed off as she glanced at Trelawny. He gave a brief nod. Then her brows knitted together in a puzzled expression as her glance swung slowly back in my direction. 'Just now you said "these acts." What did you mean? Was there more than one?'

I hesitated. 'Please believe me that I intended to tell you and Raphael this afternoon,' I began, choosing my words carefully to cause her as little additional upset as possible. Briefly, I mentioned the *cinquedea*'s appearance in my room, downplaying my own sense of alarm. 'Aside from saying goodbye to Baldini, I wanted to give him the weapon to research its history; then I intended to tell you about it.'

Paula's mouth tightened into a thin line as she swung her glance in Trelawny's direction. 'I suppose you knew about the dagger, as well.'

He nodded.

'I cannot believe, after all that we have been through on this journey, that you both would conceal something like this from me, if only for a short time.' She slammed the water glass on a nearby table, causing some of the liquid to spill on the carpet. 'It pains me almost as much as finding my room in such a shambles. You still do not trust my ability to deal with adversity, Aunt.'

'That is not so,' I protested. 'I simply wanted to keep you from fretting.'

'I can assure you that I am more than capable of handling disturbing news after the last few weeks' events.'

Her tone struck a chord in my heart. Of course, she was right. Every time I tried to conceal something from her, it rebounded on me. And I knew only too well that Paula was hardly a delicate flower. She had been raising a child without a father and doing quite well before she came to live with me.

In truth, I was probably more dependent on her than she was on me.

I will never underestimate her again.

'Ladies, perhaps we need to make amends and move on to the matter at hand,' Trelawny reminded us.

'Yes, indeed,' I agreed readily. 'I truly ask for your pardon, my dear niece.'

Paula hesitated, then rose and embraced me. 'Of course I forgive you because I never doubt your intent . . . Now, we must clean up this mess before Raphael returns with Georgiana.'

'With three of us, it should not take long.' I reached down for the suitcase which had been flung on the floor and picked up Paula's favorite white cotton dress lying alongside; its bodice had been ripped apart into several jagged pieces. *Dio mio.* Sickened at the sight of the torn lace trim that we had so lovingly sewn on to the neckline, I carefully folded the garment. Perhaps it could be mended.

Like most things in life . . .

While Trelawny righted the furniture, Paula and I stacked the torn dresses on the bed and found, luckily, two of her frocks had survived intact. Then we replaced all the unbroken knick-knacks in their original spots and tossed the broken pieces in the dustbin. Within an hour, the room appeared tidy again – just in time for Raphael's appearance with Georgiana in hand.

He scanned the results of our labor but said nothing.

'Mama!' Georgiana ran forward to briefly embrace Paula and then me. I held her close for a few moments as she chattered away excitedly about the sweets that Raphael had bought for her. '*Il cioccolato.*' She held up a small square of chocolate with a sprinkle of multicolored confetti on top before she popped it into her mouth.

'Ah, well, we must not have any more of those treats before we have tea with Contessa Teresa – it will spoil your appetite.'

'*Sì*, Mama,' she said, a little note of disappointment creeping into her voice as she gave it to Paula.

'Come, do not pout, Georgiana – I have a little surprise for you, my dear.' I motioned her over to the tea table where I had set her gift. When I handed it to her, she beamed with excitement once more.

Quickly, she skipped over to the corner and sat on the floor, the box on her lap. She untied the bow and flipped open the lid, squealing in delight as she scooped out the ball-and-cup toy and began to toss it up and down.

Once she was occupied, I turned to Raphael and whispered, 'What did the hotel manager say?'

Trelawny and Paula moved closer.

Raphael began in a low voice, 'He confessed that there have been several robberies in Ravenna recently but did not think this one might be connected—'

'Because nothing was stolen?' Paula finished for him.

'*Esattamente.* He seemed skeptical that anyone would slip into your room and simply ransack through your possessions for no other purpose. After I pressed him, he finally agreed to contact the local police, but I do not think he will try too hard to do anything about it.' A momentary look of irritation crossed Raphael's face.

'It may not matter.' Trelawny took a quick glimpse at Georgiana who was still playing happily in the corner. 'I think it is unlikely that our intruder was a local. A common thief *would* have stolen your jewelry and not taken the time to rip up your dresses – that is the work of someone who wants to send a threatening message – and who perhaps followed us here with Matteo. At any rate, I will send word ahead to Baldini about what happened, so we can speak with him when we return to Florence.'

'Oh, I almost forgot: the manager gave me this letter for you from Signora Guiccioli.' He reached into his jacket pocket and handed the folded note to me.

Breaking open the elaborate wax seal, I opened it and my mouth slowly turned upwards as I read the contents. 'She is happy to send her carriage for us later today to have tea with her again – that is at least some good news.'

'Agreed. Then, after our visit, we need to plan our next move very carefully. I know we all want to continue our quest, but the two incidents today must give us pause, especially the appearance of the *cinquedea.*'

'*Cinquedea?*' Raphael asked.

As Paula explained, he grew visibly disturbed.

'Perhaps it is best if we return to *Firenze*,' he said, drawing closer to Paula. 'I do not want you to be at further risk, *mi amore*.'

She stroked his face. 'I will be perfectly all right with you by my side.'

'Mama, look, I did it!' Georgiana triumphantly held up the cup with the ball inside of it, then she danced toward us.

As I watched her, a fiercely protective wave of love came over me, and I swept her up in my arms.

Dolce Georgiana.

I would not let anything happen to her.

'If we follow through on our request to have tea with Teresa, I think it is best that we also inform the local police we are taking a brief excursion outside the city,' I proposed, stroking Georgiana's soft curls. 'It cannot hurt.'

'Agreed,' Trelawny chimed in. 'I will do so before we leave.'

'Are you recovered enough to accompany us, Paula?' I queried, taking in her drooping eyelids.

She nodded. 'But I might take a rest before we leave and give Georgiana a chance to take a nap as well.'

Dropping a kiss on Georgiana's head, I also declared a need for time to refresh myself before our departure. It was only an hour's carriage ride to Teresa's villa south of Ravenna, but it had been an upsetting morning, to say the least.

Trelawny proposed that we assemble in the lobby in two hours after he had a chance to inform the *polizia* of our plans. As we dispersed, I hoped the respite would allow me not only to compose my emotions from the day's events but also to ready myself to meet once more with the woman who had supplanted me in Byron's life. Despite her many kindnesses extended toward me, I had conflicted feelings about seeing her in person. We lived worlds apart, except for our link to him. Certainly, we had both survived after Byron died, but, unlike me, Teresa had wealth and rank. She even had an advantageous, late-life marriage to a marquis and lived in Paris for a number of years, moving back to Ravenna only after his death. And she had the satisfaction of being Byron's last love when I was only the discarded mistress. A divide that was not easy to bridge.

But I was determined to meet with her again nonetheless – for Allegra's sake.

After having taken a fitful nap, I changed into my afternoon dress of striped taffeta and restyled my graying hair into a neat twist low on my neck. Then I donned my precious gold locket which nestled beneath the hollow of my neck. Scanning my reflection in the full-length mirror, I took in the image of my still-trim figure. No longer young but with enough vigor to see this search for my daughter through to its end.

How ironic that my hunt for Allegra had brought Teresa and me into each other's orbit, meeting for the first time only days ago, two women bonded by the man they both lost. Byron would have loved the drama of it all . . .

Off in the distance, a church bell rang twice, and I knew it was time to leave.

I arrived downstairs minutes later and found everyone waiting for me.

'You look lovely, Claire,' Trelawny murmured as he moved forward. Staring down at me, his eyes held only gentle understanding. A soft tenderness. He knew that seeing Teresa brought back painful memories for me. And in that knowledge, I felt the connection that only old friends share, all the memories and feelings built up over the years.

Ah, my friend, I wish things had been different and I could have loved you the way you deserved . . .

'Teresa's driver just arrived, but he seemed slightly unwell, so I told him to stay here at the hotel. I know the way through the Filetto forest well and can handle the carriage myself.' Trelawny inclined his head toward a heavyset, middle-aged man slumped in a chair off to the side of the lobby. His head was tilted back against the wall, revealing a pale face and drops of moisture beading on his forehead.

'Nothing serious, I hope,' I said.

Trelawny eyed him briefly. 'I doubt it, but the staff will look after him while we are gone.'

As we moved outside into the blazing afternoon sun, I

welcomed the sight of Teresa's white carriage, with its emerald-colored trim and Guiccioli crest of arms, parked out front. Admittedly, I desired its comfortable elegance.

Paula placed a hand on Trelawny's arm. 'If you do not mind the company, may Georgiana and I ride on the perch with you? She has been begging me to travel up top for ages.'

'*Per favore, Signor Trelawny?*' Georgiana tugged on his jacket as she gazed up at him.

'Of course, little one.' He tweaked her curls affectionately. 'I may even let you take the reins, if your mama approves.'

Paula smiled hesitantly. 'We shall see.'

'I suppose that leaves you and me to take the inside seats, Raphael,' I observed as he helped me up the carriage stairs. I did not mind because it would give me the chance to speak with him alone about his intentions toward Paula. Now that we had the Cades sketch and could sell it, we would finally have the financial means for Paula and him to wed. Certainly, he seemed to love Paula enough to marry her.

Once Raphael and I settled on to the green silk interior, Trelawny headed the horses down the Via Cavour and through the Porta Adriana's magnificent marble archway which led out of town. Scarcely a quarter of an hour later, the flat landscape changed to forest thickets, and I lowered the window, taking in the earthy smell of tall pine and chestnut trees, and commented, 'The woods of Filetto are quite splendid. I see why Teresa was drawn back to this spot after the marquis died – such a cool and sheltering place during the hot summer months.'

Raphael inhaled deeply. 'The ancient Romans believed the trees were inhabited by spirits from another world – sacred and not to be cut. Even now, they are untouched by human hands. *Incontaminato.*'

As Raphael chatted about the pristine woods, I surveyed his finely etched profile with the symmetry of a classic Italian statue. *Un bel viso.* Beyond that, his hair was thick and dark, his eyes the color of coal. Dressed formally today in breeches, a white shirt, and a jacket, Raphael looked quite the gentleman. I could see why Paula adored him.

He would make any woman proud, except for his poverty.

Paula and I had met Raphael when Matteo engaged him to do odd jobs around our apartment in Florence. He became our *domestico*. It did not take long for Paula and him to progress from furtive glances to a passionate love affair but, thus far, they could not marry because neither of them had the financial means to establish themselves. But that would change after I passed on some of the proceeds from selling my artwork; they would be free to wed, and love would triumph in a way it never had for me.

'You are quiet, Signora,' Raphael commented, his glance fixed on me. 'Are you thinking about our last visit with the *contessa*?'

'A little.' Leaning my head back against the velvet cushion, I tried not to remember the violent events that had occurred so recently at her villa. 'It is remarkable that Teresa agreed to see us after our last visit, but she seems to be a very . . . forgiving woman. Even so, I must confess that I slightly envy her station in life.'

'Sadly, we cannot choose the fate we have been given. I wished for so long that my parents had survived the carriage accident that took their lives and that I had been raised in the light of their love and concern. But at least I had my *nonna* until she passed away.'

'It must have pained you terribly.'

'*Sì*. It was ten years ago, but I still miss her.' His mouth tightened.

So sad to be left alone in the world at such a young age.

He would have been only sixteen at the time of her death. Lonely. Destitute. Willing to do anything to survive. For the first time, in spite of his outwardly loyal devotion to Paula, I felt tiny cautions stirring inside me as I recalled Baldini's warning earlier today:

If you had to choose one member of your circle who could be hiding some kind of sinister intent, who would it be?

Raphael?

No. It could not be him. He had put his life at risk to oppose Matteo, first in Florence and then here in Ravenna. If he had somehow been involved in my landlord's evil schemes, would he have placed himself in jeopardy by being our defender?

Still . . . 'If I may ask, Raphael, how did you manage to
survive those years all alone as a youth?'

'I took whatever jobs I could find with well-to-do families.'
He closed his eyes for a moment as if he could not bear to
look back. 'There is never a shortage of menial tasks to do
around their palazzos, from sweeping floors to cutting
firewood. I could barely support myself; it was a . . . sad
existence. *Desolato.*' His voice took on a bitter edge of hurt
and loss.

'Then you met Matteo?' I asked casually, transferring my
gaze again to the landscape of trees passing by in a slowly
unfolding line of dense foliage.

'I cannot deny that he was the one who hired me as a
domestico, no matter what he has done,' Raphael stated flatly.
'He treated me decently and paid fair wages. Your apartment
at the Palazzo Cruciato was only one of his many properties
that I looked after, so there was never any want of work.'

'After everything that has happened, it is difficult for me to
acknowledge that someone like Matteo had any good qualities,
but he was a good landlord at first, especially when he leased
the apartment to us for a rent that was half of its worth.'
Granted, the Palazzo Cruciato had been an elegant mansion
two hundred years ago, but it had passed from the original
owners' possession and been subdivided into various apartments for those who lived in 'genteel poverty' – like Paula
and me. Slightly shabby, our rooms were the only ones that
overlooked the Boboli Gardens with its lushly planted acreage
behind the Pitti Palace. I had chosen that apartment for a
specific reason: the gardens had been the site of my last meeting
with Byron when we buried Allegra's lock of hair at the base
of an obelisk – the same one that appeared in the Cades sketch.
Many days, I would sit at my window and gaze at the gardens,
remembering what had occurred there.

My final goodbye to both Byron and Allegra.

'Why do you ask, Signora?' he queried.

'No reason in particular.' Trying to reign in my misgivings,
I reminded myself that Matteo had deceived all of us, which
undoubtedly included Raphael.

Reaching across the carriage's interior, he touched my

arm. 'I hope you do not think I knew anything about Matteo's treachery. I never saw that side of him. Our relationship was based purely on business: I worked for him and that is all.'

'Just seeing you and Paula together is enough proof that you are loyal to her and me.' My voice was firm, but I did not know if I was trying to convince him or myself at this point. 'And now that we can sell the Cades sketch, there is nothing to prevent your marriage to her.'

He shifted backwards in his seat and slowly withdrew his hand. 'I wish to support Paula *myself*, not live on her money. If I cannot do that, everyone will say that I am marrying her for her wealth, which would make me nothing better than a fortune-hunter.'

'Surely not,' I protested.

'It is true; the gossips of Florence will say I am an *opportunista* – a mercenary. I know only too well that people can be cruel, especially when a young man without means ends up marrying above his station.' He traced the window's frame with his index finger. 'Like the woods of Filetto, some things never change.'

'Truly, Paula and I are hardly part of Florentine nobility or above your class – quite the contrary. We have no real social connections beyond a few British expatriate friends, for obvious reasons.' My relationship with Byron was known by most of my countrymen, even if not discussed openly in front of me. Still, I heard the whispers of scandal and disapproval that followed me everywhere; I had grown used to it over the years. 'You must not let others hold you back from a chance at happiness. *All* men deserve such hope. That is what the *Risorgimento* was all about.' I spoke with passion, having long been persuaded by both Byron and Shelley that rules were made to be broken.

'You sound like an idealist,' he commented with a short, bitter laugh. 'But I do not share that optimism. Italy might be unified, but many of the same families own much of the wealth of this country, and they wield their power over the rest of us. No, I must find my own way to support Paula and Georgiana. Anything less would be deemed dishonorable behavior.'

'Then you condemn Paula to not have her heart's true desire.'

'It is my dearest wish to be wed to her, as well, but I cannot make a home with Paula if *I* am not providing for her.' He clenched his jaw and looked away.

'But—'

'*Please*, I do not wish to discuss this matter any further.' His voice turned clipped and final.

I started to press him again but stopped myself. From his tone and posture, I could tell he would not change his mind. If I said anything else, it might even drive a wedge between Paula and him, which I would do anything to avoid. So I decided to remain silent – for now.

The carriage rolled along the next few kilometers with only the sound of wooden wheels grinding against the gravel road in a steady rhythm. When we thumped over some object in the road causing us to jerk to one side in a sudden motion, Raphael reached out to catch me from sliding off the seat. Once I righted myself again, I thanked him.

'I am always here to assist you, Signora,' he said quietly. 'Even if we disagree about some of my decisions.'

'Most appreciated.' At least, I hoped that he was still an ally, in spite of his reluctance to wed Paula. 'I thought I might ask Michael Rossetti to assist us with the sale of my sketch immediately after we arrive in Florence.'

'Of course, I am not familiar with the art world but, as a critic, Signor Rossetti probably knows quite a few collectors who might be interested in it.'

'I will write to him later today,' I vowed, adding, 'though your help in this matter would still be welcome.'

'It will be an honor.'

Whatever my cautions about Raphael, I knew I could trust Michael Rossetti. As a well-respected member of the famous literary family and friend of Trelawny, his reputation had preceded him. And after traveling to Ravenna specifically to inquire about my Byron/Shelley letters and give me the Cades sketch, he had more than proven himself to live up to that stellar renown. Even more reassuringly, he had confided that he found the drawing among the inherited possessions of his uncle – John Polidori – so he could have so easily kept the artwork for himself. I had once deemed Polidori an enemy when he was Byron's physician in Geneva during the summer of 1816, but Rossetti had restored his uncle's true character when he gifted me with the sketch which Polidori had kept for me. Admittedly, I was wrong about Polidori. And, while I gratefully accepted Rossetti's gesture, I could not have imagined that his appearance would set a complex and tragic sequence of events into action. Nor was it over yet.

One thing *was* clear: I had learned not to judge a man's true motives too quickly. In that vein, I hesitated to censure Raphael over not wanting to marry my dear Paula because his reasons could turn out to be genuine.

I would wait and see.

We completed the last part of the trip without speaking further, but the impact of his words still resonated in my thoughts. In truth, I knew very little about Raphael, except for what he had chosen to share with us, but I could not verify those facts. There may be other parts of his life that he had chosen not to reveal. Times when he might have lost his way in the fight to overcome his poverty. In that vein, surely there could be no harm in asking Baldini to make discreet inquiries about him once we returned to Florence. I had promised not to withhold any information from Paula, but until I had any real evidence that Raphael might be playing false with us, there was nothing to share . . .

The carriage halted with an abrupt jolt, shaking me out of my speculations.

We had arrived at Teresa's summer residence which had once belonged to her father: the Villa Gamba.

I swept my glance over the three-storied structure, a pleasant-looking country home, rather than a palatial estate. Made of red brick, with a tiled roof and freshly painted shutters, the villa was shaded by massive oak trees that stretched over it in graceful arches. Although I preferred the busyness of Florence's crowded streets, I could see why Teresa liked its quiet restfulness.

Teresa's footman swung open the carriage door and helped me down the steps, then Raphael alighted. As I shook out the

wrinkles in my dress, I stepped on to the elegant walkway and
turned my face toward the afternoon breeze which had cooled
the air slightly. After the sweltering journey, even the slightest
puff of wind provided welcome relief.

Trelawny jumped down from the perch, then gave a hand
to Paula and Georgiana who were laughing and chattering
away about their adventure.

The footman gestured us toward the villa, and Raphael took
the lead, clasping hands with Paula as he drew her toward the
front door. My heart gave a little tug.

'Aunt Claire, I held the reins all by myself,' Georgiana
exclaimed, motioning her hands up and down as if she were
leading the horses. 'It was so much fun.'

Trelawny swung her up in his arms, holding her against the
sky until she giggled in delight, then settling her on his chest.
'She will be an excellent horsewoman.'

Forgetting my qualms temporarily, I stroked Georgiana's
soft cheek. 'You are so fearless, my darling child.'

'Just like her great-aunt,' Trelawny added, moving forward.

I raised a brow in wry irony. As I started to trail them, I
caught sight of a blurry figure out of the corner of my eye as
he darted behind one of the oak trees. A quick-moving silhou-
ette of a man. I paused, an oddly primitive warning flaring
inside of me.

'What?' Trelawny turned, following the direction of my
glance.

'I thought I saw someone dash behind that tree near the
rose garden,' I whispered.

Trelawny slowly took stock of the area, keeping a tight grip
on Georgiana. 'Perhaps it was a yard worker.'

Seconds passed.

The air stilled as if it were holding its breath.

But no one appeared.

Unaware of anything amiss, Paula and Raphael entered the
villa, stopping only briefly to glance back for Georgiana.
Quickly, Trelawny set her down and urged her to join them.
She ran toward Paula with her arms stretched wide to hug her
mama before they disappeared inside.

Once they were safely out of sight, Trelawny reached for

the pistol at his waist and signaled for me to stay put. Then he slowly and silently moved toward the oak tree.

My nerves tensed as he edged closer.

Convent of San Giovanni, Bagnacavallo, Italy
August 1821

Allegra's story . . .

I have a visitor coming to see me.

When Sister Anna told me at first, I grew so excited, thinking that my dear papa was on his way to the convent. But it turned out to be his friend, Mr Shelley. I remembered him only slightly from the early days with my mama – a tall, funny-looking man with freckles and wild hair who always had his head buried in a book.

Still, it would be nice to see him.

Perhaps he would tell Papa how much I longed to be with him in Ravenna again.

When Mr Shelley arrived, I met him in the courtyard during the late afternoon when the sun had begun to sink low on the horizon. Waiting patiently near one of the lushly blooming flower beds, I held up the hem of my white muslin dress and curtsied as he approached.

Smiling, he held out a basket of sweetmeats and told me how I had grown into a lovely lady. I struggled to understand his English since I spoke nothing but Italian at the convent, but I sensed he approved of my quiet manner. Sister Anna had worked to tame my willful ways.

As I took a sweet from him, he asked if I liked living at the convent. I shied away from answering at first, not wanting to seem ungrateful for Sister Anna's many kindnesses, but, eventually, admitted that I often felt lonely.

'I miss Papa.'

'I know you do, but things are . . . difficult at present.' He knelt down and brushed back my hair with a soft touch. 'You must believe that he would have you with him if he could.'

Stubbornly, I kept my head down and kicked at a small pebble in the grass.

'It is true. Your papa loves you very much,' he added.

'Then why does he not visit? Or respond to my letters?' My voice sounded peevish, but I could not help it.

'He will when the time is right – I promise,' Mr Shelley asserted. 'And you must be brave just like your mama. In truth, she wanted me to tell you that she thinks about you every day and would travel here at an instant's notice if she was allowed to see you.'

'But Papa would not mind if *Mammina* came because he never denies her anything.'

Sitting back on his heels, he studied me intently. 'I meant your English mama.'

Reaching back into my memories, I envisioned a pretty lady with olive skin and sparkling dark eyes rocking me in her arms as she sang out: *My darling Allegra, sweet child of light.*

Then her face faded into nothingness . . .

'I see you still remember her.' He touched my cheek and smiled. 'Never forget your mama because she will always keep you in her heart.'

'I promise.' But I was not sure that I could live up to that vow since I barely recalled her – only snippets, without any real sense of a time or place, that would occasionally flicker through my mind. Like her singing to me. But it happened less and less often.

'She would be pleased to hear it, and I shall tell her of your pledge.' He handed me another sweet. 'In the meantime, you must learn all about great literature – especially poetry – so you will be a well-educated young woman. Do you like verse?'

'*Sì.*' I savored the sugary taste of the candy. 'Sister Anna reads the psalms to me every day, and I memorize long passages from the Bible. She says she is most pleased with my progress.'

His mouth seemed to tighten. 'I trust you read from other works, as well – especially your papa's.'

'Sometimes.' Actually, I read little else beyond the Scriptures, but I recalled Papa reading his poetry to me.

'I shall speak with her before I leave,' he said with a clipped tone. 'You are the daughter of a great poet and should know about your heritage.'

Tugging on his sleeve, I burst out, 'Take me with you, so

I can be with Papa and *he* can read his poetry to me himself. *Please.*'

As he covered my hand with his, Mr Shelley's chest heaved in a deep sigh. 'I wish I could, my dear child. There is nothing I would like better than to see you reunited with your father, but he is adamant that you remain here . . .'

'I want to go home,' I pleaded, still clutching his jacket.

'Soon, I hope.'

Defeated, I dropped my hand and spun away from him, knowing only too well what that meant. I would not be leaving the convent. My lower lip began to tremble as I struggled to control my dismay, when I wanted nothing more than to throw myself on the ground – cry and pound the earth until Mr Shelley gave in to me. But it would do no good.

'Allegra?' he said quietly.

'*Sì?*' I turned slowly as he rose to his feet.

'You must remain positive because the world is changing quickly, and your papa will do everything he can to bring you home.' He leaned down and cupped my face in his hands. 'Never forget that you are the "daughter of Earth and Water / And the nursling of the Sky . . ."'

I frowned, not understanding his words. He kissed my forehead and set the basket on the ground next to me. Then he was gone.

And I was alone once again.

FOUR

'Above or Love, Hope, Hate, or Fear,
It lives all passionless and pure:
An age shall flee like earthly year . . .'

> Byron, 'When Coldness Wraps This Suffering
> Clay,' 25–27

Ravenna, Italy
July 1873

I felt the muscles in my body tighten with each step as Trelawny inched closer to the oak tree. The lush foliage around Teresa's villa, which seemed so beautiful at first sight, had taken a dark turn. A shift into some vague threat. He moved soundlessly and slowly until he reached the tree, then disappeared behind it in a sudden motion. I drew in a sharp breath, watching the low branches sway in his wake. After a long moment, everything quieted again, but he did not reappear.

Please let Trelawny be safe.

Finally, I heard him curse as he emerged, shoving his pistol back in place.

Shaking in relief, I hurried toward him, but stopped when I saw what he carried in his left hand: a small animal, its head dangling downward, limp and lifeless.

Dead.

My hand went to my mouth as I spied the spreading patch of blood on the creature's reddish-brown coat.

'It is a baby red fox – they run wild in rural Italy, especially the northern regions.' Trelawny closed the distance between us, maintaining a tight grip on its neck. 'They like to den in woodlands, so the mother is probably lingering somewhere nearby in the Filetto forest, and not happy at his absence. We need to watch for her.'

'Should we tell Teresa in case the mother shows up?' I posed, lowering my hand.

'I think it best to inform her footman so as not to alarm her unduly.' He let it fall to the ground with a muted thud. 'The animal had already expired when I found it . . . and not from a natural death.' Kneeling down, he rolled the fox over and pointed at a gold stickpin protruding from the animal's side; the ornament's head seemed to be made of jet stone carved into the shape of a hatchet with two small rubies in the center of the blade: the kind of jewel that men used to secure their cravats.

I shuddered as all of my misgivings returned in a rapid rush of emotion. 'Do you think someone deliberately stabbed the creature?'

He gave a grim nod. 'It has been dead for hours because the body is already cold. It was killed sometime before we arrived—'

'And placed there for us to find?' I cut in, considering the figure I had just seen scurrying behind the tree.

'It is possible that you may have caught sight of him before he had the chance to position the remains; then he dropped it and ran before I could catch him.' Trelawny spat on the ground. 'Coward.'

'But why?'

'Leaving dead animals is a common way to intimidate people in many parts of Italy, and whoever did it knew we would have seen it on our way inside the villa.'

I groaned and shook my head. 'First, the *cinquedea*, then the vandalism of Paula's room, and now this horrible act of cruelty . . . I cannot take much more.'

'You must stay strong, Claire.' Trelawny stroked the fox's soft fur with the back of his hand. 'We cannot give in to fear and intimidation, even though this poor creature of the wild deserved better than to be trapped and killed so viciously.'

As we stared down at its still form, I heard Paula's laughter drift out of the villa – soft and light. Then she called out for us to join them. I responded that we would be there directly, gazing over to make certain she was not standing near the open window and could see us. 'You need to dispose of the fox before anyone else sees it. I do not want to further alarm Paula after what happened this morning.'

'Nor I.' He stood up, picking up the animal and seizing the stickpin. 'You might not want to look at this, Claire.'

'I have seen worse,' I said firmly. 'Do what you have to.'

In one quick motion, Trelawny pulled out the stickpin and covered the wound with his hand. Blood gushed through his fingers but he held on to the fox until it bled out; then he loosened his grip and handed me the stickpin. 'Give me a few minutes to hide the carcass in the underbrush.'

He strode away, and I gazed down at the stickpin in my palm, flinching at the scarlet stain on rich gold. In spite of the head's odd hatchet shape, it hardly looked lethal. More a piece of gentleman's finery than an instrument of death, which somehow made it seem even more sinister.

I leaned down and wiped the stickpin against the grass beneath my feet until it gleamed again. Sorting through my bag, I found a cotton handkerchief to wrap around the pin, and carefully placed it inside, making certain that the point was covered by the cloth. By the time Trelawny reappeared, I had finished my clean-up task.

'Are you ready to go inside?' he inquired.

'Not really, but we cannot remain out here any longer because Paula and Raphael will grow suspicious.' I smoothed back my hair, noting only a small tremor in my fingers. 'We will have to tell them later—'

'Aunt Claire, we are about to have tea,' Paula exclaimed, now standing in the open window. 'What are you two doing?'

Waving at her, I smiled widely. 'Just admiring the landscape – it is quite lovely.'

'It is way too hot for you to linger in the sun,' she chided us. 'Please come in.'

'You know how your aunt cannot resist the beauty of nature,' Trelawny exclaimed. He nudged me forward gently as he murmured, 'Take heart . . . I shall be at your side.'

I gave a brief nod of gratitude.

My dear Trelawny . . . always there for me.

We entered the villa's elegant main hall with its high ceiling and marble floors – dominated by a stone staircase that curved along one wall in a graceful sweep like a marble wing. Exquisite and refined. A lady's house. It had passed through many generations, reflecting the old wealth of Teresa's family. Sadly, she was the last of her line since her brother, Pietro, died young and she had no children. The house would pass to strangers.

As we strolled into the parlor, I spied Teresa seated on a rosewood settee near the fireplace, its empty hearth decorated with a basket of wildflowers. When she saw us, she broke into a wide, generous smile. '*Buongiorno.*' Her delicate, petite figure appeared almost doll-like with her white hair and smooth, pearly skin.

'*Salve, Contessa,*' I replied, noting that Paula and Raphael sat comfortably in matching chairs off to the side, with Georgiana on the floor, playing contentedly with her cup and ball. A cozy scene. So sweet. So normal. It helped to focus on them as I tried to push aside the images of the dead fox. *Do not dwell on its death. Paula will know something is wrong.*

Our hostess asked my niece in Italian to pour the tea from a porcelain tea service already set in front of her and then continued, 'I am so pleased that you have joined me again this afternoon.'

I took the seat next to her. 'Even after the dreadful events of our last visit?'

'But that was not your fault, and the killer was brought to justice. It could have turned out very differently, and I am grateful that God intervened through the quick action of Signors Baldini and Trelawny.' She crossed herself and murmured a short prayer of thanks. 'In spite of the turmoil, I welcome your presence once more.'

'You are most generous, Contessa, especially after the events a few days ago when we brought such mayhem into your life. I truly had no idea that Matteo had followed us here with such malicious intent.' I avoided looking at the spot where Trelawny had wrestled on the floor with Matteo and ended up fatally stabbing him, but I still remembered how the blood had splattered on the carpet when he fell. And I could still hear his shriek of pain when the blade pierced his chest. I closed my eyes briefly. It had been a horrific scene. 'We placed you in great danger, and for that I am truly sorry.'

'*Accetto le tue scuse.*' She inclined her head as she accepted my apology. 'At this stage of my life, the days have become quite long, and I miss the . . . excitement of family and friends from the past, though I would not want to experience such a life-and-death struggle again. It is always painful to see a man die, even one so loathsome.'

'Indeed, I think we brought a little too much *eccitazione* to your beautiful villa.' Pushing all thoughts of Matteo's demise out of my mind, my gaze moved to the table next to her where a small curio stood: an oval-shaped frame that held Byron's image with a wild and windswept look, painted during his years in Ravenna. When I had first seen it in Teresa's parlor, I felt a twinge of jealousy that she possessed such a memento of the man I loved heart and soul, but now, after meeting her, I found it simply a reminder of his presence. He had brought together both of our lives in a chaotic, violent way that I could not have imagined. In that silent reflection, I heard his voice inside of me, saying, *You see why Teresa also stirred my heart? She is charitable, even in the face of peril.*

As I focused back on her, I noticed calm acceptance in her eyes.

'You forget, Signora, that my father and brother were revolutionaries, men of great passion and commitment to the *Risorgimento*, and I have lived through turbulent times in Italy. I learned to put unpleasant events behind me, no matter how great the loss.' Teresa shrugged in that Italian way that simply accepted life with all of its great joys and terrible tragedies. Not resignation – just acknowledgment. It was an attitude that I could never cultivate since I found the moments of happiness all too brief, giving way to long seasons of discontent. I wanted the joyful times to never end.

Paula handed me a cup of tea, and I inhaled the strong, pungent smell of oolong, my favorite brew, which I had first tried during my youth in Geneva. I had preferred its rich taste ever since and had mentioned it to Teresa on our last visit. She had obviously not forgotten.

Then my niece passed around the *ciambellone*, a lemon-flavored Italian cake in the shape of a large donut with a tart and moist texture. After finishing her duties, Paula lifted Georgiana on to her lap and handed her a piece of cake.

Teresa helped herself to a small section of the dessert. 'But you must tell me about your visit with Sister Anna. Did she have anything helpful to pass on about Allegra?'

'To a certain extent, yes.' I replaced the delicate cup on its saucer. 'Initially, she apologized for not revealing her true identity to us and said it was because of her shame and guilt, but her explanation seemed a bit contrived. I did not press her since she confessed that she had been present when Allegra, along with several other of her young students, fell ill. All but one of them died and, sadly, she believed that my daughter succumbed to typhus along with the other young ladies . . .' My voice broke as images of Allegra lying ill in her bed rose up in my mind – her tiny face pale and feverish. A twinge of pain tugged at me even now, knowing that I was not with her during those difficult days, no matter what had been the outcome. As her mother, I should have been there to nurse her.

Teresa's expression stilled and grew solemn. 'I am so sorry, Signora. I had hoped Sister Anna might have passed on more hopeful news.'

'I did as well.'

'And she offered nothing else?' Teresa asked.

'Only that Tita had traveled to the convent during the epidemic and was the one who took away Allegra's remains.' I refilled my cup.

Drawing back, Teresa's eyes widened. 'But how could that be when he was banished at the time? I know for certain because he was arrested after a violent incident outside Pisa that included both Byron and Shelley. Tita and my footman, Antonio, were questioned by the *polizia*; my servant was released, but Tita was tried and sentenced to exile. So it is unlikely that he could have journeyed to Bagnacavallo.' She glanced at Trelawny. 'You would recollect that, of course.'

'Indeed, yes, and I told Claire as much,' he hastened to explain. 'Sadly, when that event in Pisa occurred, I had already left for Rome and knew nothing about it – or what had been done about Allegra.'

'Signora, do you recall what Byron did when he heard about Allegra's illness?' I pressed her.

She hesitated. 'I . . . I was staying at the Palazzo Parri near Byron's residence when he heard that Allegra had contracted typhus. Directly after that, I believe he sent word to a physician from Ravenna to attend to her. He grew quite concerned over her health, but the doctor related that Allegra's fever was "light and slow," and he had full confidence in her recovery. I prayed for her but heard nothing else until a few days later when Pietro told me Byron received the news that Allegra had suddenly passed away. He was overcome with grief, collapsing on to a sofa where he remained for an hour or more. No consolation could reach his heart. No words of love could assuage his grief. Later, he shut himself in his rooms for days, refusing to see anyone.' She picked up the curio with Byron's image and sighed. 'At least, that was the story I heard. There were many parts of his life which he hid from me.'

And me.

Byron always seemed as if he shared every innermost thought, but he often hid his true feelings . . . and actions.

Paula shifted Georgiana on to the thick oriental carpet on the floor, handing her another piece of *ciambellone*. 'Is it possible that Byron sent someone else – a friend – who managed to smuggle out Allegra?'

She replaced the small portrait on the table, her fingers lingering around the oval frame. 'I can only say that he loved her dearly and would have done anything to protect her, even if it meant deceiving all of us.'

I took a long sip of my tea, reflecting on her last comment. If Byron had, indeed, faked Allegra's death as he told Trelawny, whether carried out by Tita or someone else, he had concealed it from everyone. And after our two meetings with Teresa, the person closest to Byron and Allegra during that time in Ravenna, I had nowhere else to turn. She was my last hope to corroborate Trelawny's recounting of Byron's late-life confession about our daughter.

Another blind alley.

Somewhat defeated, I recalled the lines from Shelley's favorite work, *Prometheus Unbound*, to strengthen me: *Hope creates from its own wreck the thing it contemplates.* But I could not summon the Titan's strength in this moment. It felt too difficult in the face of yet another disappointment.

Teresa transferred her gaze to me once more, sad and pensive. 'Byron did tell me later that he had your daughter's remains taken to Livorno for passage to England, whether that was true or not.'

If so, for burial at St Mary's Church in Harrow-on-the-Hill – without my ever having seen her.

Even more upsetting, the rector at St Mary's had refused to place a plaque on Allegra's grave because of her illegitimacy, although he allowed her to be buried at the entrance of the church. So much for charity. An innocent child was denied a proper burial and religious services because of the sins of her father – and mother.

Everyone fell silent for a few moments, with only the sound of Georgiana humming happily as she nibbled on her cake, blissfully unaware of the heaviness that had descended on the room.

'Did anyone deliver a message to Byron to confirm Allegra's passage?' Trelawny finally spoke up.

Teresa tapped her cheek. 'I . . . I do not think so, but I remember a priest came to Pisa to see Byron after the events at Bagnacavallo. He stayed overnight at Byron's palazzo but left the next day before I had the chance to receive him.'

'Did you ever hear the priest's name?' I asked, my thoughts tumbling in sudden agitation.

'No – Byron never spoke about him to me.' Teresa blinked several times. 'But Pietro thought Byron mentioned to him that the priest was in attendance at Allegra's deathbed. Do you think he was with Tita?'

'It certainly seems more than coincidental that he appeared only a few days after Tita may or may not have been at the convent to tend to Allegra.' My fingers curled into the folds of my dress, crumpling the material into wrinkled balls.

'And it would not be far-fetched to think he might have conspired with Tita to hide Allegra's fate and conceal her in

Livorno,' Trelawny added. 'When Byron told me that Allegra survived, he never outlined how he actually managed to carry out the deception. It had to be an elaborate plan, executed with only those men whom he could trust. I wish he had filled in the blank spaces.'

Raphael coughed audibly. 'Where does that leave us, then?'

'I am not sure.' As if on cue, the gilt ormolu clock on Teresa's fireplace mantle chimed with five light rings – a sweet and somber reminder that it was time to begin the trip back to Ravenna. Still, I wanted to linger in case she recalled some other clue, a fragment of a conversation or a line from a long-lost letter.

Something.

Anything.

'There are always options, Claire,' Trelawny reassured me.

'Indeed, and we have already taken up too much of Signora Guiccioli's afternoon.' I set my cup on the tea table with a sense of finality.

'It has been my pleasure.' Her features softened with the warmth and grace of a woman steeped in generations of hospitality, further enhanced by a long lifetime of shared *largesse*.

I rose from my chair and kissed her cheeks in the Italian manner and, for the first time, I noticed the faint outline of bluish circles under her eyes and the papery texture to her skin. *This is the last time I shall ever see her in this world.* I would miss her . . . not only because she was one of the last living links to Byron but because she had been a good mother to Allegra in my absence. Her *mammina*.

She studied me for a few seconds. 'I would urge you not to give up on your search for Allegra. We Italians believe in miracles, and I shall pray for one.'

'*Grazie, Contessa.*' We both seemed to know that whatever forces had brought us together, we would always have this kinship forged by a desire to right a wrong from the distant past – our past. Then I stepped back, and an invisible curtain seemed to fall between us, signaling the last moment of humanity we would share together in this life. The final act.

Afterward, our little coterie bade farewell to Teresa, and we quietly exited the villa together. I took one parting glance at its red brick walls glowing in the afternoon sunlight, imagining all the seasons that had unfolded as Teresa's family had filled the walls with laughter and tears. *La gioia della vita.*

Paula touched my arm. 'Aunt, I think Georgiana needs to stretch her legs a bit before we start the journey back to Ravenna. Would you mind if Raphael and I took her for a brief walk around the garden?'

'Not at all.' I slid my eyes toward Trelawny who gave an imperceptible nod.

As Paula and Raphael strolled off, heads bent to whisper something between them while Georgiana skipped alongside, I scanned the grounds uneasily.

Trelawny leaned down and murmured, 'Trust me, whoever left the dead fox is long gone. They are safe.'

'Even so, let us keep them in sight.' As I watched their retreating figures, my concern over their safety faded, but the radiance of young love that seemed to encircle them had dimmed somewhat after my talk with Raphael. *Could we truly trust him?*

'What is it, Claire?' Trelawny interrupted my unpleasant musings. 'I know that look only too well. Do you question what Teresa shared with us?'

'No, it is something else entirely.' I took a few moments to gather my thoughts and summon the courage to relate what Raphael had shared with me. 'During the journey here, Raphael revealed more details of his relationship with Matteo; apparently, it goes back much longer and is much more complex than I had previously guessed. Our landlord was his benefactor, not just his employer. Raphael assured me he was not part of Matteo's scheme, but for the first time I found myself questioning the honesty of his heart – especially after Baldini warned this morning that someone close to me may have placed the *cinquedea* in my room. I now find myself wondering if he truly loves Paula?'

'But, Claire—'

'Please, let me finish.' I held up a hand. 'Raphael also said he has no intention of marrying Paula, no matter how much money the Cades sketch brings us, because he wants to be able to support her entirely on his own; anything less he believes would label him as a "fortune-hunter" by Florentine society. I was quite taken aback and not sure I believe his excuse for not wanting to wed her. Do you think he is playing her false to "assist" me with the sale of the drawing, then take the money for himself and disappear? I would willingly share the proceeds with Paula and him, but perhaps he wants *all* of it.'

Trelawny leveled a fleeting look in Raphael's direction and then made a dismissive gesture. 'I think we would have noticed some type of suspicious behavior the past couple of weeks. In fact, he has risked his life twice over to protect you and Paula . . . I doubt whether he would have done that if he had dark motives. And he was honest with you today on both counts – hardly the actions of a man who is playing a waiting game to cheat you.'

'But can we be certain?'

'Not entirely, I suppose,' he said. 'All we rely on is what is on the outside, and his actions have been beyond reproach. Even though the connection to Matteo warrants some caution, I am still inclined to place my trust in Raphael.'

'You are undoubtedly right, but with everything that has happened in Ravenna, I am questioning my own shadow at this point.' I hesitated, blinking with bewilderment. 'And today was beyond the pale with the dagger, the ransacked room, and now the dead fox. I never thought I would say this, but perhaps we need to reconsider moving forward on our quest.' My heart sank a little even hearing myself say the words, as if I had already made an admission of defeat.

His brows rose. 'You do not wish to journey to Livorno?'

'I . . . I am not sure.' The afternoon breeze picked up again, causing my skin to prickle as tiny bits of dust blew around me. 'Until we know who might be behind these violent threats, it might be best to return to Florence, sell the sketch, and see if Lieutenant Baldini has any information on the *cinquedea* or Raphael. I cannot allow Paula and Georgiana to be placed in jeopardy any further.'

A probing query came into his eyes. 'Perhaps we should ask Paula herself.'

'I know what she will say, yet the prudent course seems

best – for now.' Observing Paula and Raphael moving back toward us, I saw him edge along a flower bed of pink and white roses with Georgiana in tow. Paula leaned down and plucked one pearl-colored rose that had drooped in the sun, then tucked it into her daughter's hair. *A sweet tableau.*

Trelawny adjusted his stance, shifting his weight to the back foot. 'We should not be suspicious of the young man based solely on a conjecture of Lieutenant Baldini. As a police officer, he is naturally mistrustful of everyone. But he did not provide any real evidence that Raphael has done anything *wrong*.' He emphasized the last word. 'Still, I suppose it is not unreasonable to delay the next stage of our journey until we have confirmed his good intentions.'

'A brief respite, then?'

'If that is what you wish.' His tone still echoed reluctance. 'All I have wanted on this journey is to redeem myself for the deception that Byron asked me to carry out . . . and help you find Allegra.'

I placed my hand on his arm. 'You have more than proven yourself, Edward, during these last few weeks, and I have forgiven you with my whole heart.'

'That is all I need to hear.' He exhaled a long sigh of contentment as he reached for my hand and pressed his lips against the palm. 'I can ask no more . . . except that you grant Raphael a similar chance to show his true character. He has earned that and more.'

Weighing his request, I had to admit that it was more than fair. 'I shall keep my mind open for now.'

'About what?' Paula queried as she approached. Raphael lagged behind with Georgiana now perched on his shoulder as she sprinkled rose petals on his hair.

Trelawny released my hand.

'The . . . possibility that we should suspend our search for Allegra,' I said, without embellishment or apology; my niece would see either of those as evidence of my wavering resolve. 'Please believe me, I do not make this suggestion lightly, but it may be the wisest choice until Lieutenant Baldini can investigate the recent events.'

Her mouth formed a small circle of surprise. 'I know we

said that we would plan our next step after speaking with Teresa, but I think this decision is somewhat hasty. You want simply to return to Florence?'

'Yes, I do,' I said, resolved. 'Someone else has grown increasingly bold in his attempts to threaten us, and it is alarming. Perhaps we have taken too many risks over the last couple of weeks, and it is time to be sensible.'

'If you are doing this because of Georgiana and me, I ask you to reconsider,' she pleaded. 'We all vowed to see this quest to its end, no matter what, and I want to honor that commitment to you. Besides, Raphael and Trelawny have protected us thus far, and I trust them to do so in the future—'

'Paula, I must ask you to defer to my judgment in this matter.' I noticed Raphael drawing closer, lowering Georgiana to the ground as he took his place next to my niece.

'Has something happened?' he inquired.

'My aunt has determined that we are to return to Florence and will hear no opposition,' she blurted out. 'Raphael, you must persuade her that is the wrong course of action, nothing more than defeat, and that is not an acceptable option.'

Paula waited but, when she saw that Raphael would not comply, she gave an exclamation of impatience and flounced off with Georgiana in hand.

'*Scusami*,' Raphael said before he hurried after Paula, urging her to stop, but she waved him off.

'Paula has your impetuous nature, but I believe she will come around eventually,' Trelawny observed once we were alone again. 'She came on this adventure for love of you, and that will also guide her to acceptance of your decision.'

I tossed a wry grimace at him. 'Love never caused her father or me to acquiesce, so I am not sure my niece will find that quality within herself either.' My dear older brother, Charles, would take me in when my exploits turned sour and help me to start over, rarely asking for explanations and always providing a temporary shelter until I found a new situation. He had his share of adventures as well, and I mourned him deeply when he died.

'Sometimes duty and respect are enough to make amends, especially between generations.'

I fingered the locket at my throat and traced the etchings around its heart-shaped rim, remembering my own mother. A cold, unbending parent who disapproved of my impulsive nature that, ironically, was so similar to her own rash youth which drove her into the arms of my unknown father. I managed to brush aside our past conflicts when she became too old and infirm to care for herself. But we never shared our secrets. I never told her about her granddaughter and she never revealed my father's identity. Near the end, when Mama was dying of a nervous fever, she gave me the only gift she had ever passed on: the gold locket that I wore every day. A last memento.

'By fits and starts, I suppose I found my way.' I released the locket.

'And Paula will do the same.' He gently nudged me toward the carriage. 'Maybe on the road back to Ravenna, you can persuade her to your way of thinking.'

When hell freezes over . . .

After Trelawny gathered everyone again, he settled Paula, Georgiana, and me inside the carriage, while he and Raphael climbed on to the high perch to drive the horses.

Once we set out, my niece handed Georgiana her china doll and then flipped open Trelawny's book of Byron's poetry and pretended to focus intently on the page – signaling that she had no intention of engaging in any conversation. So I remained mute as the brittle silence between us grew as oppressive as the heat. To distract myself, I slid open the window and turned my face to the changing landscape. Mercifully, the air gradually cooled as we headed through the Filetto woods, and I breathed in the strong pine scent, catching sight of the late-afternoon sun flickering between the trees – light then shadow, shimmering in pale streams.

Georgiana tugged on my dress to recapture my attention, and I saw her grimace as she attempted to place a cotton bonnet on her doll's head. It kept slipping off. Gently, I took it from her, fixed the bonnet in place, and tied the ribbons in a bow. As I passed it back to her, I murmured, 'Perhaps your mama would like to read some of Byron's poetry aloud?'

Paula did not respond.

'Yes, please,' Georgiana urged.

'His work is not suitable for a child,' she responded in a short, clipped tone. 'It is about wicked men who do not respect women.'

Georgiana's face drooped in response to Paula's sharp retort.

'Surely not all of the verse is improper,' I pointed out. '*Childe Harold's Pilgrimage* and *The Prophecy of Dante* are about love and heroism.'

Without responding or looking up, she turned the page with a forceful snap.

Suitably rebuffed, I gave my attention to Georgiana again while she played with her doll, humming under her breath as she arranged the wispy curls around its hand-painted china face. After a little while, she abandoned that activity, nestled into the crook of my arm, and gradually fell asleep. Her breathing grew deep and regular, and I gazed at her tiny face, so soft and sweet in response; my heart swelled with the same intense love I had felt for Allegra. A powerful longing to see her grow to maturity and have a beautiful life.

I had failed a child once but would not do so again.

'Paula?' I whispered, reaching out to her. 'Will you please stop this behavior, for Georgiana's sake?'

She lowered the volume and moved her head slowly from side to side, then raised the book again.

I gave up, knowing Paula's stubborn nature only too well. She would eventually relent, but not at present.

Our carriage rolled along in a soothing rhythm; I focused on the tall pines which drifted by outside and refused to rethink my decision. How many times had I begun a new journey and watched the landscape, not knowing what would await me when I reached my destination? Too many to count. Always driven by my passion for adventure, I kept moving, never staying in one place for too long. Sometimes disappointed, sometimes elated, I never hesitated to take risks – until now.

Of course, I would have remained in Geneva forever with Byron if he had agreed to raise Allegra with me.

That haunted summer of 1816 seemed to hold the key to what happened to my daughter, but I could not recall a definite event that seemed to foreshadow why Byron had hidden her fate from me.

Except for that one afternoon . . .

I was lounging under the striped awning of the Villa Diodati with Shelley and Mary, while he read aloud passages of Rousseau's novel *Julie* and Mary sketched the lake. For once, the constant stream of thunderstorms had abated and I watched the sun drop slowly behind the mountains off to the west, splashing streaks of red and yellow across the sky. Breathtakingly beautiful. I was already pregnant with Byron's child.

Allegra.

Byron emerged from the villa, conversing with a young man who had the look of a poet himself, wearing an open-collared shirt and breeches. They laughed at something Byron said before he introduced the newcomer as Ludovico di Breme, a young poet and revolutionary, recently arrived from Ravenna. I murmured a polite greeting to him in Italian, and he bowed. But as he straightened, his face changed and became curious, as if he had seen something unexpected. It made me slightly nervous, and I could only think he had heard the gossip in Geneva about my relationship with Byron. I turned away and spoke to Mary, but I could feel his furtive regard until they strolled back inside the villa.

On their way, Byron's hand brushed against my neck, and I could still feel the passionate touch of his fingers. Then they moved on as di Breme took one last glance over his shoulder in my direction.

An oddly primitive warning had sounded within me.

Only recently, Trelawny confessed that Byron, too, had been concerned about di Breme's fixation on me – especially when, shortly after his appearance, an unknown assailant pushed me down the stairs at Castle Chillon. Unfortunately, no one could connect di Breme with the attempt on my life. Oddly, when Byron moved to Italy and became a member of the Carbonari, he kept up his acquaintance with di Breme and, later, suspected his servant of plotting to harm Allegra.

None of it made sense.

Closing my eyes to blot out these perplexing visions, I felt myself relaxing into the gentle rocking of the carriage and slipping into a reverie . . .

I stood near the shore of Lake Geneva under a clear blue sky.

Young and happy, I twirled around in the sunlight, singing one of Byron's favorite Irish melodies, 'Sing, Sweep Harp.' While he watched me, Mary and Shelley looked after their infant son, William, who crawled around on a linen blanket spread upon the ground. The day was perfect after a month of unrelenting rain – warm and summery – and I raised my voice in joy, letting the pure notes ring out.

. . . the midnight air

Among thy chords doth sigh,

As if it sought some echo there—

Just then, a loud clap of thunder pierced the quiet of our halcyon day, and I froze.

Quickly, Mary lifted William into her arms, nodding her head in the direction of Mont Blanc, but its snow-capped peaks gave no hint of a coming storm.

Nonetheless, Shelley gathered up their things, and they hurried off toward the Maison Chapuis, leaving only Byron and me. He held out his hand, and I eagerly ran toward him. But the moment before our fingers touched, he pulled back. After a long moment, he turned and walked slowly toward the Villa Diodati. I cried out, but he did not stop. Frantically, I tried to follow him, but my legs refused to move.

Then, I was alone.

Come back, my love . . .

'Aunt Claire, wake up.' A voice came from far away, echoing through my mind.

As I gradually came back to consciousness, I felt someone shaking me lightly – and I awoke fully to behold Paula's cold face.

'You fell into a slumber about an hour ago,' she said shortly, closing her book. 'It seemed as if you were quite agitated.'

'Just a bad dream – nothing more.' Trying to gather my wits, I realized the carriage had stopped.

Glancing out of the window, I spied the Al Cappello's majestic presence through the twilight; two gas sconces had been lit on either side of its entrance, illuminating the doorway with a pale, flickering yellow light. Just then, Trelawny swung the carriage door open. He helped Paula and Georgiana descend the steps and, without a word, my niece drew her daughter inside the hotel, followed by Raphael. Sighing, I let Trelawny help me to exit the carriage.

'Still no sign of capitulation?' he inquired, escorting me through the open doorway and into the lobby. It was deserted, except for the young manager who lounged behind his desk, idly scanning the guest ledger.

'None.'

'Give her time.' He led me to the staircase and halted. 'It has been a long day. Perhaps you need to see if you still feel the same in the morning.'

'Yes, I shall take supper in my room and consider it.' I lingered for a few moments. 'Thank you, Edward.'

'My pleasure.' He smiled down at me, and a tiny stir of affection passed between us like a soft whisper of two souls. 'I will find Teresa's driver to see if he is well enough to return the carriage to her villa . . . then you can let me know tomorrow about the travel arrangements, but do not fret too much over Paula.'

'I shall try.'

After he took his leave, I slowly made my way up the stairs and let myself into my room. Scanning it quickly, everything looked normal, refreshed by the staff with the chair cushions plumped and curtains drawn against the dark. A bouquet of flowers sat on the writing desk, filling the air with a delicate fragrance.

I set my bag on the tea table, taking a few moments to absorb the still, quiet atmosphere. But jarring scenes of the day flitted through my mind: the *cinquedea*'s sharp blade, the shredded dresses in Paula's room, and, finally, the dead fox outside Teresa's villa. Violent, disturbing images. Daggers and blood.

Dear God, why was all of this happening?

I thought this journey to Ravenna and Bagnacavallo would finally lay all my ghosts from the past to rest – one way or the other. But not so. With no concrete evidence about Allegra's fate, we were still being threatened by some unknown assailant who dogged our every step. Never presenting himself, but never fading completely away. Perhaps all I had to do was abandon my quest and perhaps the world would right itself again.

If the abbess had provided something of real substance to indicate Allegra had survived, I might feel differently about giving in to Paula's urgings to keep moving forward, but she had not. She was convinced Allegra had died. And no one else was still alive from that time to verify Byron's confession about Allegra's fate. They were long dead.

Then my eye fell on the bundle of Pietro's correspondence, still neatly stacked on the table. At least his letters contained recollections of a time when they were all still alive, a lingering trace of what was real and true.

As a last hope, I reached for them.

At sea aboard the Hercules
July 1823

My dearest Teresa,

I know parting from Byron and me was a wrenching time. Already, I miss you more than I can say, my sister. I find myself thinking of our years together as children, wandering the pine forests of Filetto, never believing our childhood paradise would end. But it did, and though we have been expelled from Eden, I believe fighting for Greek liberty will restore my hope after our dream of a free Italia *died.*

We are sailing south down the coast to Cephalonia, then eventually onto Greece.

From the outset of our voyage, Trelawny and Tita have been restless, firing pistols off the stern, but Byron remains quiet and reflective. He speaks of his great love for you constantly . . . do not think that he has forgotten you. I know his notes may seem short, but he is occupied with so many great matters that the London Greek Committee has given him – the fate of Greece is in his hands.

And the situation that awaits us is complicated.

Byron writes letter after letter to the Greek leaders. Sometimes, he is optimistic and sometimes in despair but, through everything, he knows what we learned from the Carbonari insurrection: resolve and unity will win the day; conflict and division will end in defeat.

But the Greeks are divided into three factions now: the territorial leaders who wish to keep their little fiefdoms, the warlords who command their own armies, and the westernized exiles who have returned to Greece, ready for battle. Byron tries mightily to bring them all together to fight the Turks, but they must put aside their personal desires for the great cause. I am not sure that is possible.

I fervently hope they will choose the road to victory . . .

The breezes at sea are warm and strong during the day, not much cooler at night. Nevertheless, we are steadily making our way to Cephalonia; once we arrive, Byron will make plans to launch a naval force to unite these Greeks at a stalemate with each other. It is a task fraught with difficulty and distress, but I know Byron will manage it.

For now, we sail on.

We spent two days in harbor at Livorno to load supplies on the ship, and I found myself growing impatient to continue our journey. But Byron spent the time ashore attending to business that he did not reveal to me. On the morning we departed, I saw him bidding farewell to the same priest who visited the Casa Lanfranchi in Pisa as he handed over a large, leather money pouch. I found the exchange curious but did not inquire about it.

At the same time, we took on board a passenger who calls himself Captain Vitalis, yet he appears to have no Greek military rank and travels with only one companion – an Italian. Byron said they asked to join our voyage to travel to Greece, which seems unusual when they could have easily booked a direct passage. The Italian is quiet and respectful, but there is something quite odd about Vitalis in the way he shadows Byron, listening to his every conversation. When we were on the deck, watching Trelawny shoot a duck suspended from the mainyard of the mast, I spied Vitalis writing furtively in a corner; he

shoved the paper in his pocket when he saw I was
watching him. I suppose it is to be expected that there
are spies everywhere from the different factions, but
something about him makes me very wary.

I shared my suspicions with Byron, and he said he
would keep an eye on Vitalis.

Still, I was not completely reassured.

On a happier note, we passed the beautiful islands
of Elba and Corsica yesterday, which I have never seen
before; I was told that the islands were once connected
and, indeed, they look very similar, with their mountains
rising up from rocky coastlines. Byron spent the evening
talking about Napoleon's imprisonment at Elba,
expressing both admiration and distaste for the deceased
dictator, then reciting lines from his 'Ode to Napoleon'
which stirred my heart and made me imagine the defeated
exile's lonely existence:

Then haste thee to thy sullen Isle
And gaze upon the sea;
That element may meet thy smile –
It ne'er was ruled by thee!

Byron said he did not want to be a leader like Napoleon
who could not lay his sword aside. Instead, he wanted
to emulate his hero, George Washington, and wondered
if the Greeks would view him like the great American
leader, a man driven by principle and honor.

I think it will be so . . .

We are now heading toward Sicily where I hope to see
Mount Etna. I have heard the volcano produces a smoky,
thick cloud and could erupt at any time, so I eagerly look
forward to seeing it . . . then on to Cephalonia where
the edge of war awaits us.

I can only say once again, dear sister, that I miss
you more than anything. Our little world on board ship
is pleasant, often full of high spirits, but I catch Byron
looking off into the distant seas every so often, and I
know he is thinking of all that he has left behind in

Italy – and everything he has lost. He sometimes mentions Allegra as though she were still among the living, then his eyes tear over as he acknowledges her passing. So sad that the child died at such a young age.

But I promise you we shall make you proud when we finally arrive in Greece. You will know that all your sacrifices have been for a higher purpose.

Ti amo,

Pietro

FIVE

'It is the hour when from the boughs
The nightingale's high note is heard . . .'

Byron, 'It Is the Hour,' 1–2

Ravenna, Italy
July 1873

I clutched the letter and stared ahead, trying to brush aside
the veil between the present and past, to see everything
that Pietro had described.

All this time, I never knew anything about life aboard the
Hercules. It was the type of man's world that Byron enjoyed,
occupied with shooting and boxing and swimming. He reveled
in those kinds of activities where women were excluded,
relaxing in a way that he never could around females who
watched his every move with obsessive fascination as if he
stepped out of the lines of his own poetry – the Byronic hero
in the flesh. Fame carried such a price for him. Only among
other men could he let his guard down. Of course, I rarely
saw that side of him during the summer in Geneva;
only glimpses flashed through his self-protective shell when
Shelley would coax him into good humor. Then it felt as if
the world brightened.

But that never lasted very long.

I would have boarded the *Hercules* with him, sailed into
the fray of revolution, and braved every danger by his and
Trelawny's side. But I was never given the chance. When I
once wrote to Byron that I would have preferred to be his
friend rather than his lover, it was true to some extent; I wanted
to share his life of freedom and adventure. Sadly, that sort of
existence was not permitted to young women, even though I

always pushed against those restrictions with every fiber of my being.

It made life difficult, but never dull.

Taking a few minutes to reread Pietro's letter, I imagined myself on the deck of the *Hercules* with its pleasant diversions, almost able to taste the salty sea breeze against my face . . . then my fantasy halted abruptly when I scanned the lines again about the priest at Livorno. Teresa said a priest had also visited Byron in Pisa immediately after Allegra supposedly died. Could he be the same holy man whom Byron met in Livorno? And who was Captain Vitalis? I had never heard Trelawny mention his name, although Pietro felt the need to mention him to Teresa – along with the fact that Vitalis seemed a disturbing presence on the ship: *Something about him makes me very wary . . .*

Sliding on to the bed, I set the letter aside, trying to sort through some of the more puzzling sections of Pietro's narrative. While the mood aboard the Hercules seemed high-spirited, there were obviously moments of caution and suspicion. They were, after all, a band of revolutionaries who understood the dangers of their expedition. So why would Vitalis and his companion join them, knowing they were at risk?

I stared up at the coffered ceiling with its richly carved wooden squares, each one with a rosette in the center. But I found no answers in the intricate pattern.

Yawning, I realized that I was too tired to think about it any further. As I began to fold the yellowed parchment letter, I noticed the ink had blurred on the passages that referenced Byron's love for Teresa. Had she wept when she read it, her tears dropping on to the letter with a sense of grief and loss? Not just for Byron's demise, but also for the brother who died only three years later.

At least Pietro's narrative described a further connection to Livorno: the priest. It seemed significant that Byron had taken time from his last voyage to meet with him in the port from which Allegra's remains had supposedly been sent back to England – and the same city where Antonia Gianelli, the lone survivor of the convent's typhus epidemic, had been taken. Mere coincidences?

Possibly.

But I was beginning to believe that Livorno held the key to what actually happened to my daughter. And it might be my last chance to find any answers. Maybe, just maybe, I should rethink my decision to give up the quest – as long as Paula and Georgiana could be protected. I did not take the fox incident lightly, but the port city beckoned almost irresistibly . . .

The next morning, I arose early but completed my toilette slowly while I planned what needed to be done before we departed Ravenna: find a seamstress to repair some of Paula's dresses, pack my luggage, and plan our next destination. I had a busy day ahead. After donning a blue cotton dress, I finished off with a velvet ribbon threaded in two loops through my plaited hair.

First, I needed to speak with Paula.

Quickly, I made my way downstairs to the dining room, now deserted except for our little band of travelers enjoying a light breakfast of bread and tea at a table near the large front window. Paula sat next to Raphael, while Trelawny lounged across from them with Georgiana on his lap; he was trying to feed her a small piece of crusty bread. As I entered, they all smiled at me, except for my niece. She kept her face stubbornly averted.

'*Buongiorno.*' I slid on to a chair at the head of the table and placed a napkin in my lap. 'I am glad that all of you waited for me because I have something to share with you.'

Trelawny looked up curiously.

I poured myself a cup of oolong tea, savoring the slightly bitter brew for a few seconds before I began. 'I had a surprising revelation when I returned to my room last night and read one of Pietro Gamba's letters – a note that he wrote to Teresa when he and Byron were *en route* with you to Cephalonia aboard the *Hercules.*' I gestured with my cup in Trelawny's direction.

'Ah, yes, we were all on fire about the Greek revolution and could barely contain our excitement as we made our way along the Italian shore,' he responded, brushing the crumbs off Georgiana's mouth. 'So young and naive . . .'

Paula made a scoffing sound. 'Men and their wars – such selfish recklessness. Then we women must always contend with the aftermath.'

'But fighting for one's freedom is a worthy cause,' Raphael protested. '*Italia* would never have been unified without those who died during the *Risorgimento* so we might enjoy our liberty. *Eroismo.*'

'I suppose so.' She shrugged dismissively at his definition of heroism. 'But men should think about the consequences of their actions. Everyone should. All decisions should be considered carefully, taking others into account, especially those who have fully committed to a particular course of action.'

Of course, she was referring to me.

Taking another swallow of my tea, I set the china cup in its saucer. 'In fact, I agree with Paula, which is why I would like to propose one last destination, if all of you concur.'

Instantly, she swung her head in my direction. 'You have changed your mind?'

'I am . . . considering it,' I said tentatively. 'Pietro's letter about their voyage caused me to believe that we might want to travel on to Livorno after a short stop in Florence—'

'*Brava!*' Paula beamed a radiant smile at me. 'What did Pietro say to convince you? Do tell us everything, Aunt.'

'I am most curious as well,' Trelawny said drily, now holding a cup to Georgiana's mouth so she could drink her tea. 'Especially when I do not remember anything of importance happening on the *Hercules* that related to Allegra.'

Taking in a deep breath, I laid my hands on the table, spreading my fingers across the white lace tablecloth, my slightly wrinkled skin standing out against the pale, delicate material; then I related the details of Pietro's account of the events in Livorno – especially the part about Byron meeting with the same priest who had come to Pisa directly after Allegra's demise. 'So what do you think? Does it seem unusual that Byron would meet the priest in Livorno and apparently give him a sizeable sum of money?'

'Most definitely,' Paula responded quickly, then prompted Trelawny to answer.

'It is noteworthy, but strange that neither Pietro nor Byron ever mentioned the priest to me during the entire trip, and they certainly had many opportunities during the ten days it took to reach Cephalonia.' Lifting Georgiana from his lap, he

placed her gently on to the floor. She skipped over to the
mahogany sideboard where she helped herself to another piece
of bread. 'It is possible Byron was giving a donation to his
basilica.'

'In Livorno?' I made a scoffing sound deep in my throat.
'Certainly, Pietro did not seem to think the priest's appearance
was out of the ordinary, but he found the money exchange
rather peculiar,' I supplied. 'Do you think it is mere happenstance that Byron, who detested religion, took valuable time
out of preparations to not only meet with the priest, but to
hand over some type of payment? I doubt it. Surely their
meeting must have held more significance.'

'It does seem . . . interesting.' Trelawny sat back, his eyes
flickering in reflection. 'We have little else to go on, and I
am willing to pursue every possibility, no matter how
insignificant.'

Raphael nodded his assent.

'Trelawny, what about the passenger you took on in Livorno:
Captain Vitalis?' I queried as I picked absently at the lace in
the tablecloth. 'Did you notice anything suspicious about his
behavior during his time aboard the ship?'

'Not really. In fact, he seemed a comical figure for the
most part, and Byron delighted in teasing him.' Trelawny
buttered the piece of thick, crusty bread that Georgiana had
brought back to the table. 'Vitalis introduced himself with
letters of support from a Greek patriot living in the city,
asking if we would allow him passage on the *Hercules* to
his village in Greece. Then, he sailed with us to Cephalonia
but left the expedition there. If anything, Vitalis was too
intrusive for Byron's taste – always showing up when any
of us appeared on deck, wanting to be part of every activity,
even when none of us particularly desired to include him.
And I suspect he was always writing in his journal because
he, like many, wanted to record every moment linked to
Byron for some future publication, featuring himself in a
prominent role, of course.'

I resisted smiling, aware that his own *Recollections of the
Last Days of Shelley and Byron* had been a popular if sometimes slightly embellished account of his role in their lives.

'Maybe Pietro saw something about Captain Vitalis that you did not,' Raphael chimed in. 'What happened to him after he departed?'

'I do not know exactly since I had gone ahead to Tripolitza when Byron landed in Missolonghi.' Trelawny handed the bread back to Georgiana and rubbed her head affectionately. 'Everyone assumed he made his way home on his own.'

I digested this account, wondering as I had many times in my life how two people could have such different impressions when it came to taking stock of a man's nature, but, then again, most everything seemed to be filtered by our experiences and feelings. Reality could take many forms. Sometimes clear, sometimes blurred. Always contradictory.

In this instance, I found Pietro's observations more intriguing – and promising. 'It is probably a fool's errand to travel to Livorno, but it feels like our only choice at this point. Still, with the two incidents that happened at the hotel yesterday, I would understand if you were hesitant about journeying on. I am cautious, as well . . .'

'We must at least give it a try,' Paula urged. 'I would like to know what the priest did with the money.'

Trelawny nodded slowly. 'Once we arrive, I will follow up on my inquiry with my old friend at the bank to see if he can find any record of a priest arranging funds to care for a child in April 1822; he might be able to help us. Also, I have been thinking about the abbess's admission that Antonia's parents took her back to their home in Livorno. It might also be worth having him research whether she still resides in the vicinity or not. Even though many years have elapsed, Antonia may have at least some vague memories of Allegra's last days at the convent.'

'It is almost too much to hope for such an outcome.' My heart gave a little lurch of excitement. 'And you, Raphael? Will you continue on with us?' I questioned, watching carefully for his reaction.

'*Certamente.*' He smiled easily. 'I will do as Paula wishes in all things.'

I folded my hands. 'Then we are decided. We leave tomorrow for Florence, and then on to Livorno.'

Trelawny proposed we journey along the *Via Firenze*, the southern route to Florence, and then on to Livorno. 'It should take us perhaps only two days since it is a well-traveled road through the *Foreste Casentinesi* with coaching inns all along the way. I know it well.'

'I am happy to assist you,' Raphael said, 'since we are short of time.'

Paula leaned into him. 'You are always so wonderfully dependable.'

Yes, so it would seem.

'If you both could make the arrangements, we can be ready to set out in the morning.' Reaching for the teapot, I poured myself another cup of tea, filling it almost to the brim. I needed fortification for the busy day ahead. Certainly, I had proposed this ambitious journey, but I also found that the actual details seemed a bit daunting. Trelawny excelled at this type of intricate organization of travel routes and coaching inns.

Paula suggested that she and I purchase items from the food market for lunch the next day on the road, to which I readily agreed. Then Trelawny and Raphael took their leave to make the travel plans. After they exited, Paula and I chatted about our upcoming tasks today, while Georgiana nibbled the last of her buttered bread.

I slid another cup of tea across the table toward Georgiana who gulped it down. 'Paula, I know you did not wish to abandon our quest and, much as I want to continue, I also do not want to see Georgiana put in harm's way. If you wish to remain with her in Florence, I can travel with Trelawny—'

'No, we must all stay together,' she said, her arm sliding around her daughter in an inclusive embrace. 'I would give my life for Georgiana but, at this point, after seeing my room ransacked and not knowing who was responsible, I think it is best if we remain protected by Trelawny and Raphael. There is no one else whom we can trust.'

I hesitated. 'Are you certain?'

'Yes.' She leaned her cheek against the top of Georgiana's head. 'There is strength in unity. Remember when you took us in, when I had nowhere else to turn? It did not take long for us to bond as a family, and we must keep those ties intact. I am sorry that I was short with you before. I feel so passionately that we must not allow ourselves to be intimidated into abandoning our quest. We must be strong, for Allegra's sake.'

Tears stung at my eyes. 'Oh, my dear, I am so proud to call you my niece . . .'

She raised her head and smiled.

My whole being swelled with love in that moment of harmony between us again. We were of one mind. Perhaps it would not last long with two women as strong-willed as us, but, for now, it was enough to know we had regained the unified resolve and purpose that would see us through this last stage of our journey together – and beyond.

Paula drained her teacup and rose in one fluid motion. 'If we want to leave tomorrow, we should start packing, though I have fewer dresses to attend to than I did a few days ago.'

An image of ripped cotton and silk flashed through my mind and I shuddered. 'I will ask if the hotel manager knows of a local seamstress who can mend some of the least damaged frocks overnight; we can drop off the gowns on our way to the market.'

'Let us first see which ones might be worth salvaging.' After wiping some stray breadcrumbs from Georgiana's hands, Paula led her daughter out of the dining room.

For a few moments, I sat motionless and gazed out of the front window. In truth, I feared the end of my search for Allegra almost as eagerly as I had anticipated it. All my dreams would either be realized or destroyed, and I would have to live with the aftermath for the rest of my days.

A gamble, at best.

Mid-thought, I became distracted by a young woman strolling by the outside of the hotel: she held a roughly woven straw basket in one hand and a little girl by the other one. The child whined about wanting her *bambolotto*, but her mother pulled her along, muttering in Italian that her doll would be waiting for her at home. Following their antics until they disappeared out of sight, I saw myself and Allegra in my mind's eye, during the many instances when she would throw a tantrum on the streets of London, her tiny face set in mulish defiance as she refused to obey me. Now, I would give the world to be with her again, no matter how naughtily she behaved.

Truthfully, the good and bad times do not signify after the cherished ones are gone.

Only that they had once graced our lives.

Gradually, my vision cleared, and I sighed, knowing that I could not revise what had occurred in the past.

But the future might hold a vision of hope that I once deemed forever lost.

Shortly before noon, Paula and I had sorted through her torn dresses and chosen three that could be mended: two pale-colored day dresses and a deep-cream silk evening gown. They were some of her newer frocks and had held up through the savage attack, though they would probably require some delicate stitching to be presentable once again. We carefully folded a muslin cloth around them, and I carried them downstairs while Paula dropped off Georgiana with Raphael.

Once I reached the lobby, I asked the hotel manager for the name of a local seamstress, and he suggested Signora Elisa – the wife of Gaetano, the toymaker. I agreed readily, since I remembered the beautifully embroidered curtain in her husband's shop and thought it might be her handiwork. After he gave me directions to her address, on the nearby Piazza del Popolo, he promised to send a quick note to her first so she would be expecting us. I gave him a grateful smile and then strolled over to a loveseat near the entrance. Sliding on to the thick cushions, I set the dresses next to me and waited for Paula.

The mahogany longcase clock in the lobby began to clang on the stroke of noon and had reached only half a dozen chimes when my niece appeared, tucking up her hair at the back with one hand and clutching a straw market basket in the other. 'I apologize, Aunt, but Georgiana decided to turn fussy when I left her with Raphael. She knows he will give her *fritole*, and I did not protest since we have three long days of travel ahead of us. I do not want to begin our trip with her already in a rebellious mood.'

'Good choice.' Rising, I handed Paula the stack of dresses. 'Georgiana is a headstrong child, but it has been a chaotic couple of weeks, which has not helped calm her disposition. Let us give her a little leeway today because it will make the carriage ride tomorrow more pleasant.'

'And quiet,' she added with a short laugh.

I raised my hands to heaven in mock appeal as we moved toward the front entrance, giving her the name and address of the seamstress and suggesting we stop there first since the market was near the piazza. As we stepped on to the street, I squinted in the bright midday sun, noting that Italian shop-keepers were already closing up for the typically long, leisurely lunch. 'We might be able to reach Signora Elisa before she locks her doors.'

Hurrying along the Via Novembre, we reached the Piazza del Popolo a few minutes later and scanned the square lined with Venetian-style buildings. At one end, a magnificent cream-colored palazzo, flanked by two marble columns, took up almost the entire block, dominating the piazza with its sheer size and exotic facade. The rest of the structures scattered around the square were considerably smaller and in various states of disrepair. Spotting the address, I pointed at a two-storied house with a flat roof and Moorish-shaped windows.

As we drew closer, an elderly woman wearing a long, striped apron around her plump torso appeared in the open doorway and waved us forward. She disappeared inside and we followed her into a dark, cramped space, filled with long bolts of jewel-toned fabrics stacked atop each other: shimmering silks, thick velvets, and finely woven cottons.

I heard Paula take in a sharp breath as I made our introductions.

'I have never seen such beautiful material,' my niece said, a touch of awe in her voice as she spun around the room, taking in the array of textiles.

Elisa ran her fingers lightly over an emerald-green velvet gown on a mannequin, its bodice embroidered with a delicate bouquet of scrolling flowers. 'This fabric is from my hometown of Nuoro, Sardinia. They produce the most elegant velvet in all of Italy because their craftsmen learned the secret of weaving from Kashmiri merchants. It lies in the threads and the loom.' Her accent had a slight northern Italian flavor, but I could understand her well enough.

'And you added the embroidery?' I posed, noting the fine needlework of each flower stem and petal, the stitches neat and even. Never one to possess the patience for such accomplished work, I could only admire those with the skills I could never master. 'It is exquisite.'

'*Grazie, Signora.*'

'Your artistry rivals your husband's woodcarving.' I touched the beadwork along the gown's low-cut neckline. 'I bought a wooden toy from him yesterday for my niece's daughter; she was delighted with it.'

Elisa inclined her head at the compliment. 'How may I help you? The *gestore* at your hotel told me you needed some mending to be completed quickly.'

'By the morning – if possible.' Paula set her dresses on the worktable, spreading out the torn garments. 'I apologize for the lateness of our request, but we are returning to Florence tomorrow and need these dresses repaired before we leave.'

She picked up each one and inspected the garment carefully, holding it up to the light streaming in from the window and turning it around to see all sides. 'I can sew up the torn sections and perhaps add a bit of lace over the new seams, but the dresses will not look . . . *pristino.*'

'I understand,' Paula assured her. 'But can you make them wearable again?'

'*Sì.* I can do that.' Elisa spread out the dresses on her table, then turned to the shelf behind her that held hundreds of wooden bobbins with a rainbow of colors from pale pink to deep brown. 'May I ask what happened to the dresses?'

'Someone ransacked my niece's room at the hotel, including most of her wardrobe,' I said frankly. 'The culprit has not been caught, nor do we know why he did it.'

'Perhaps he was looking for valuables,' Signora Elisa commented as she selected several bobbins and began matching threads to Paula's blue morning dress. 'Ravenna is a poor city. Even though it was once the jewel of the Byzantine empire, similar to Venice, those days are long gone. The lagoons have turned to swamps, and malaria outbreaks made the city known as "the tomb of tombs." *Triste.* The trade routes moved north and the city has been left isolated and alone for centuries.' She sighed. 'Then the decades of conflict before the *Risorgimento* caused many of our young men to leave to fight with the Piedmontese. Any British tourist would seem rich – and fair game – to those of us left.'

'We are hardly wealthy,' I pointed out.

'One need not possess much to have more than a typical Ravennese,' she said calmly as she laid out three threads in slightly different shades of blue. After a few moments, she chose the middle one, then sorted through more bobbins to match the other two dresses. 'I shall pray to *Santo Cristoforo* for your safe return to Florence; the patron saint of travel always watches over those who need his protection on their journeys, especially if they journey on dangerous paths.'

Our perils were many . . .

'I shall have the garments delivered to the Al Cappello by nine o'clock tomorrow morning.' She set each matching thread atop its dress. 'Will that be acceptable?'

'Perfectly. And I cannot thank you enough for helping us.' Breathing a sigh of relief, I reached inside my bag as I asked her for the charge.

She held up a hand. 'This is my gift to you—'

'Absolutely not, Signora,' I protested. 'We cannot accept such charity, no matter how kindly it is given. We must pay you for your work.'

Placing her hands on her generously curved hips, she stood firm. 'I insist . . . and hope my offer will make amends to you for the treatment you have received in my city; it does not reflect the rest of us.'

I wavered, but the unyielding set of her features persuaded me to relent. Obviously, Elisa was not a woman to be challenged once she had made up her mind. '*Grazie mille.*'

With a brief nod of satisfaction, she scooped up the dresses and tucked them under her arm. 'I will not disappoint you.'

We exchanged a few more pleasantries, then Paula and I bid the signora farewell and moved toward the front door. Passing the beautiful green gown again, I could not help but take one last glance at it. I could almost hear the rustle of the wide skirt across a ballroom floor, elegant and mysterious like whispers on a moonless night.

Then something caught my eye.

A gold pocket-watch chain with a small, pyramid-shaped jade fob pinned to the bodice.

The small charm dangling at one end had a lovely, translucent quality that complemented the gown. Almost exotic. Then I looked closer at the fob and noted a tiny hatchet carved in the center.

Startled, I pulled back, realizing that it was the same symbol on the stickpin used to kill the fox outside Teresa's villa.

'Is something wrong?' Signora Elisa queried.

Pointing at the fob, I turned to her. 'This is such a unique ornament. Does it belong to your husband?'

'No, I bought it in a local shop.' She unfastened the pin at the other end of the chain and handed it to me. 'The jade has a thin crack along the top part of the pyramid which makes it almost worthless, so I bought it for only a few *lire*. Still, I thought it would make a temporary adornment to the bodice to inspire me while I finished the dress. I shall remove it, of course, before I deliver the gown to my client, and melt down the gold.'

'That would be a shame.' Holding the fob in my palm, it felt surprisingly weighty. 'Do you know what this little hatchet symbol means? It is . . . unusual.'

Her lips thinned slightly.

'Signora?' I pressed.

'It is a symbol used by the Carbonari many years ago.' She took back the piece and regarded it silently for a long moment. 'The hatchet designated a "master" who was in charge of "apprentices" – much like a general who commanded his troops, except they fought in the dim corners and alleyways. And the symbol was also a warning to anyone who might think of betraying them: he would forfeit his life.'

Paula gasped.

I was less shocked since I had read Byron's journal from his days in Ravenna during the *rivoluzione* of 1820. The city had been rife with stabbings and shootings, including the

Austrian military officer who had been injured outside the Palazzo Guiccioli and later died in Byron's study. Conflicted about the bloodlust that had been unleashed, Byron noted the soldier's demise in an entry that echoed through my mind: *I could still mourn that some men had to die for others to be free.*

Everyone had to choose sides, and few were spared.

In Byron's recollections, he even noted that Pietro knifed a man who had turned traitor to the Carbonari.

I shivered at the memory of violence and death.

The twin horrors of warfare.

Elisa pocketed the chain and fob. 'It is best not to bring up those things since old hatreds die hard. Many of us lost loved ones. The Ravennese were split into two factions: those who wanted independence, many of whom were members of the Carbonari, and those who sided with the Austrian oppressors. It was a terrible time, with assassinations on both sides.'

'I understand.' Everything connected to Allegra's fate harkened back to that time of the Carbonari in Ravenna, and the stickpin used to kill the fox seemed to be the most direct threat to our lives thus far. I needed to take another look at it – now. That other symbol next to the hatchet, which I could not decipher, might provide another bit of information. 'We have already taken up too much of your day, Signora. Thank you, again.'

Nudging Paula toward the door, we exited the shop without further ado.

'Aunt, what is the urgency?' Paula queried as we started down the hot and deserted street, fanning ourselves vigorously. 'I think Elisa had more to tell us about the fob, and it could have some bearing on what is happening to us now. The Carbonari cast a long shadow in Italy, and some remnants of that group might bear a grudge toward anyone connected with Byron. The reason for our visit has no doubt spread around the city, and there may be old enemies of his who still live in the area. They may have been in hiding and have now come out—'

'To take their revenge on us,' I finished for her as we passed an old man who sat on a step, scrubbing the stone with a pail of water and hard-bristled brush. 'I had not thought about that, but it could be very true. Allegra may have been their target years ago, and we are in their sights now because of something that happened with the Carbonari. But what? And why have they come forward after half a lifetime of silence?'

'I cannot fathom it.' She pulled her skirt aside from the splash of water on the sidewalk.

'Nor I.' We turned on to the Via Novembre and, a bit winded by the heat, I begged off stopping at the market with her. Besides, I wanted to look over that stickpin while the symbol on the watch fob was fresh in my mind. She set out in the opposite direction, swinging her straw basket.

Once back in my hotel room, I sat in front of the desk where I had secured my most precious belongings. Unlocking it, I slid open the top drawer to find my Byron/Shelley letters in their neat stack and the Cades sketch in its carefully rolled-up position . . . but nothing else.

Where was the stickpin?

It appeared to be missing.

Convent of San Giovanni, Bagnacavallo, Italy
October 1821

Allegra's story . . .

I am so happy.

At last, Papa is coming to visit!

When Sister Anna told me last night, I could barely sleep. I had almost given up hope that he would ever want to see me again, believing that I lost his love forever. But all changed once I knew he would be here tomorrow and then take me home with him.

My papa. My dear papa.

He has not forgotten about me.

He still cares for me.

Too excited to sleep, I awakened early this morning and dashed to the window, watching the sun rise over the clustered houses of Bagnacavallo, casting its light over the entire town. In spite of the fall's chill, it felt like a fresh dawn of happiness. My little world at the convent had turned bright with cheer and hope. Leaning my head against the window, I traced where I had etched my initials in the glass and sighed contently in the knowledge that I would leave the convent with Papa. Nothing would be left of my time here except those initials.

AB.

Allegra Byron.

I had cut those letters into the glass one afternoon when I was daydreaming about the future, when I would no longer be shut off from the outside world, but I despaired that it would never come. And no one could hear my inner cries of sadness, so I had scratched at the window like a bird clawing at its cage.

But now I would be free, and with my beloved papa.

Mia cucciola.

That is what he called me – his little puppy.

By mid-morning, I had all of my belongings packed and sat on the bed, dressed in the pink wool frock that Papa had given to me.

And I waited . . .

Lunchtime came, but I could not calm myself to eat, so I stayed in my room, praying to the Madonna for patience. Later, Sister Anna brought up a tray of hard-crusted bread and *pecorino* for me, but when I asked her if Papa had arrived yet, she just shook her head silently. After she left, I nibbled on the hard white cheese as I stared out of the window again.

Where was he?

I reminded myself that Papa was always late, always distracted. He wrote poetry long after midnight, rose in the early afternoon, and often had the servants delay his meals. Our life in Ravenna unfolded in that jumbled kind of way because Papa did not like schedules and his attention shifted like the winds.

I never knew what the day would bring – except that it would be diverting.

Having lived like that, it made convent life seem even more dull. The same dreary routine – prayers, meals, and learning by rote. Every day unfolded like the one before it, and nothing broke the sameness. I hated it.

But all of that was over.

I would be able to take up my old disorderly life in Ravenna again – with all of the people whom I loved.

Like *Mammina*.

She would tuck me into bed and sing softly to me until I fell asleep at night.

Like Tita.

He would lift me in his arms and let me pull on his dark beard until he grunted in pain. I knew he was pretending, but it was our little secret. Then he would give me a chocolate *fritole* and laugh.

Papa and *Mammina* and Tita. They were my whole world.

Il mio mondo intero.

So I waited some more.

Hours passed . . . the sun began to drop low on the horizon, but still no sign of Papa.

What had happened to him?

All summer, I had been longing for Papa to take me home, but that season had come and gone. Now, it was autumn. I could not spend a whole winter in this place.

Still sitting on the bed, my spirits drooped like the trees in the garden below, their branches heavy with leaves of red and gold and yellow. The cold winds were already sweeping in from the north, and I feared the coming days.

The dark time.

To divert myself, I began humming *Mammina*'s nightly song: *Farfallina.* The butterfly. I, too, wanted to stretch my wings.

> *Farfallina*
> *Bella e bianca*
> *Vola, vola*
> *Mai si stanca . . .*

> Butterfly
> Beautiful and white
> Fly and fly
> Never get tired . . .

I thought if only I could fly away with Papa. I would be happy for the rest of my life, knowing I would never have to return here. Then I remembered Sister Anna and felt guilty since she had shown me only kindness. Always smiling. Forever giving. I would miss her, but I could write letters so she knew I would never forget her.

Standing up, I stretched my arms to the ceiling, imagining they were wings, waving them up and down, as if I could fly. But I could not. Slowly, I dropped them, feeling the tears well up in my eyes.

Papa was not coming. He had changed his mind.

Why?

Did he no longer love me?

My heart aching in defeat, I walked over to where my trunk stood at the end of my bed, raised the lid, and started to unpack my clothes. There was no point in waiting any longer.

As I carefully unfolded a silk frock, I froze when I heard a familiar voice outside the door.

'*Allegrina?*'

Throwing the dress aside, I ran to the door and flung it open. 'Papa!' I hugged him tightly, afraid that he would vanish like a phantom in a dream. But when he dropped a kiss on my head and brushed back my hair, my fears dissolved. He was real.

As I glanced up, I saw him look over his shoulder before he urged me back inside my room. Closing the door behind us, he limped over to a chair, eased down on the seat with his club foot stretched out in front, and reached out to me. 'I have missed you so much, *mia cucciola.*'

'I have missed you, too, Papa.' Seizing his hand, I kissed it, then scanned his dear face. A little fear crept inside me when I saw how old and tired he seemed now. His eyes sad and haunted. His body thin, almost frail. 'Are you well?'

He gave a short laugh. 'Of course I am. It was just a long ride to the convent today – with a nasty chill in the air. But it was worth braving the elements to see you again. Never doubt it.'

'But you did not answer my letters,' I protested.

'I wanted to, believe me.' His voice broke as he brushed

back my hair. 'I cherished every word that you wrote. I simply could not respond. It was too . . . difficult.'

'What do you mean?'

He frowned, causing a deep furrow between his brows. 'The world is shifting rapidly outside these convent walls, and I have few people I can trust with my letters . . . yet over the last few months, I composed them in my mind every day. When I sat in my study, I even penned a few notes to you, but I later burned them because they might have been found by someone who would use them against me. Enemies lurk everywhere, especially since the rebellion failed.'

'*Sì, Papa.*' Before I came to the convent, he had been accused of being a *traditore* – a traitor – and I had overheard Tita say the Austrian police watched our house. But surely that time had passed.

'If only I could make you understand.' He touched his forehead against mine briefly and his skin felt cold. 'Know that I love you more than life itself, and your safety is the only thing that matters. I must always let that guide me, even if it causes pain for both of us.'

'But we are together now, and I am ready to go home to Ravenna. It has been so lonely here without you and *Mammina* that I could barely stand it.' Quickly, I moved over to the trunk, tossed the dress back in, and slammed the lid shut. 'All of my things are packed, and I am ready.'

He did not move from the chair.

'Papa?'

Dropping his head to his chest, he heaved with a deep sigh. '*Allegrina*, I need to explain something to you.'

Feeling that sense of fear ignite inside me again, I hesitated. Then Papa raised his head and motioned me over to him. I took a few steps in his direction, then held back as I saw the anguish in his eyes.

No.

He rose awkwardly from the chair and came over to the bed, patting the mattress as he settled on to it. 'Come here, child, because I do not have much time.'

'What do you mean?' Reluctantly, I took my place next to him. 'I want to leave with you.'

His arm slid around me in a tight embrace, and I buried myself against his chest, begging him to take me away from here.

'Stop, please,' he urged, gently stroking my back for a few minutes until I turned quiet once more. 'I came tonight at great peril because you are, and always will be, my most beloved daughter for whom I would risk the world. I have never forgotten you for one minute, and I want more than anything to take you with me. There is nothing I would like better than to see you playing in the courtyard of the palazzo on your wooden horse . . . I dream about that time, and all those evenings when you would sing for me after dinner in a voice so like your mama's – Beauty's daughter.' He paused. 'But I cannot, at least not now.'

I began weeping. 'I will die if I stay here.'

He pulled back and took me by the arms, staring at me intently. 'Never say that, *Allegrina*. You will live a long life filled with happiness and, eventually, have children of your own who will bring you such joy. Even though I may not share it with you, I will hold you in my heart forever.'

'I do not believe you.' Shaking my head, I averted my eyes.

'It is true.' He turned my face toward him. 'And I promise that you will not be at the convent much longer; I need to make arrangements for you to be taken to a secure place and, afterwards, I will join you there. It will be our new home, even better than Ravenna. You just have to wait a little longer.'

His words fell on my ears like a bone-chilling freeze, blanketing all of my hopes under an icy despair.

'You must trust me,' he added, his voice thick with emotion.

Stubbornly, I refused to answer, keeping my gaze on the floor.

'*Allegrina?* I do not wish to depart like this—'

A quiet knock on the door interrupted him, and I turned to see Sister Anna step inside, holding a candle.

'It is time,' she said in a hushed voice.

Papa nodded, then hugged me fiercely for a few moments. '*Ti amo* – forever.' He lurched off the bed, stumbling toward

the door. Then I heard him mutter something to Sister Anna
. . . and he was gone.

Papa had left me again.

I sank to the floor, crushed and beaten.

SIX

'To soar from earth and find all fears
Lost in thy light – eternity!'

Byron, 'If That High World,' 7–8

Ravenna, Italy
July 1873

W*here was that stickpin?*
I shuffled frantically through the drawer's contents, pulling out the letters and obelisk sketch, then shoving around the loose sheets of paper. No sign of it. Replacing the items, I slammed the desk drawer shut, then rummaged through the rest of the drawers. Nothing. I slumped into a nearby chair and gave an exclamation of frustration. How could a thief have broken into my room yet again when the hotel manager was having the hallway watched so carefully? He had assured me my belongings were safe.

A hollow promise.

As I banged my palm on the desk in frustration, I spied a crystal paperweight on top, which had a note peeping out from underneath. Quickly, I retrieved it and recognized Trelawny's familiar handwriting:

> Dear Claire,
> While you were out, I made some inquiries as to who might know about the stickpin and was given the name of a local artisan. I am going to visit him and hope to have more information for you when I return by midday.
> Yours,
> Trelawny

Exhaling in relief, I set the letter on the desk again. My things were safe. And I would not speculate on how Trelawny was able to obtain the stickpin from a locked desk. He had many talents, not the least of which was a doggedness that would simply not accept defeat. He never gave up on anything – including me. By all rights, a woman of my age should be spending her days in a quiet retreat, but that type of existence held no attraction for me, especially with Allegra's fate still unresolved.

Glancing at the mantel clock, I drummed my fingers on the desktop, impatient for Trelawny to return. We had little time to spare before our departure, and this might be our last chance to find some kind of connection between the recent events. The ransacked room. The dagger. The dead animal. All such menacing but seemingly unconnected acts that suggested evil had followed us to Ravenna.

Shifting uneasily in my chair, I pushed the unpleasant images from my thoughts. Nothing would be gained from such musings except to make the long journey ahead even more unsettling. It was best to think only of the comfort that awaited us when we reached the familiar surroundings of the Palazzo Cruiciato in Florence. Being there again would strengthen me for what else lay ahead. At the very least, I could see the Boboli Gardens again from my window and remind myself why I had begun this enterprise: for Allegra.

My beloved daughter.

Always and forever.

A familiar knock interrupted my reflections, and I moved quickly to the door. As I swung it open, I smiled. Trelawny. 'I have been waiting anxiously for your return since I saw your note.' Motioning him inside, I closed the door and pointed toward the sitting area.

'I would rather stand since I am still somewhat shaken by the morning's events.' He paced across the room, halting by the empty fireplace as he leaned one arm along the white marble mantle. 'I apologize for taking so long, but the man I visited had quite a story to tell about his life and . . . the Carbonari.'

'Who was it?'

'Gaetano – the toymaker.'

'That kindly old man was a revolutionary?' I exclaimed in disbelief. 'What did he tell you?' I seated myself on the settee, curling my hands into tight fists of anticipation.

'It is quite a story.' Trelawny reached into his pocket and retrieved the stickpin. He held it up, turning it around and around between his index finger and thumb. 'After you left this morning, I was thinking about this piece and remembered something that Byron told me about the Carbonari using jewelry with symbols to signal to each other. So I pilfered it before I went to arrange for the carriage; I asked the men who work with the horses if they knew of any old revolutionaries who still lived in the area. Stable boys are always a good source of information because they see everything, but no one notices them. Anyway, Gaetano's name came up. They also mentioned that a ring or pin would secretly show the man's membership and rank within his *turba*. This jeweled stickpin would have been worn by a—'

'Grand Master,' I cut in quickly.

Abruptly, he stopped twirling it. 'How did you know?'

'Gaetano's wife, Signora Elisa – the local seamstress. Paula and I went by her shop, and I spied a pocket-watch fob with the same hatchet etching on it. When I questioned her, she admitted it was a Carbonari symbol but that people rarely spoke about such things today: too many hard feelings still lingered after the *Risorgimento*. I sensed she knew more than she shared with me, but I could not cajole anything else out of her.'

'Surprisingly, after I asked to meet with him, Gaetano agreed and was very . . . forthcoming. In fact, there was something slightly too familiar about him – as if he already knew me and was aware of why we had come to Ravenna.' With a slight tremor in his hand, Trelawny set the stickpin on the tea table in front of me and regarded it mutely for a few moments – deadly quiet.

'I have never seen you quite like this, Edward,' I said, growing more concerned as his silence stretched on.

'Yes. There was much about his story that unnerved me. It

seems that there were an endless number of defectors in the Carbonari, traitors to their own brothers who disappeared when peace was declared and turned up later in wars abroad as vicious mercenaries.' Still staring down, his voice hardened. 'I have met that kind of man often over the years – totally without honor.'

Warily, I picked up the ornament, running my fingers along the carved jet hatchet to trace the smooth edges that outlined the blade and handle. Then I touched the blood-colored rubies, full of depth and fire. So beautiful, yet somehow sinister. 'Please . . . continue.'

'When I showed Gaetano the stickpin, he recognized it immediately as belonging to one of the Grand Masters of the Ravenna Carbonari because of the rubies; apparently, only a leader would wear such gems. And he had seen it before when he was an apprentice under one of them: Count Alborghetti – a member of the Papal Legation, but also a powerful figure in the Carbonari who was known for his ruthlessness when it came to anyone who turned traitor.' Trelawny came forward with a couple of rapid steps, then seated himself in the chair next to me. 'Those men simply disappeared.'

'Dear God,' I whispered, imagining all too well the violent end that these men would meet in some dark, narrow alleyway.

'Justice was swift for informants – silent and savage.' He made a slicing motion across his throat. 'Anyway, Gaetano also confessed that Byron's involvement with the Carbonari was an open secret in Ravenna; all of the locals knew he commanded his own *turba* and brought in other British expatriates to help him prepare for battles, including . . . Polidori, who made several trips here with arms and ammunition.'

I took in a quick, sharp breath. 'I had heard he followed Byron to Italy, but somehow he never impressed me as the type of man who would risk his life for a cause.' I turned very still as I summoned the image of Byron's physician who had traveled with him throughout Europe for a short period: tall and slim, with wild curls that artfully framed his delicate features.

Dr John Polidori: the uncle of Michael Rossetti.

I had believed for so long that Polidori was my enemy

during that haunted summer of 1816, conspiring to injure and separate me from Byron forever. But I had been so wrong. After Mr Rossetti gave me Polidori's journal, I realized he had just been an ambitious young man caught up in Byron's glittering orbit – or so he had recorded. There were some entries in Italy that had suspicious omissions.

Was it possible he had become a revolutionary, as well?

'There is more.' Trelawny leaned forward with a fixed, deliberate gaze. 'Byron and Polidori were often spotted in the company of two men, one of whom was rumored to be the other Grand Master of Ravenna . . . Ludovico di Breme. A quartet of conspirators.'

My hand moved my locket in a reflexive grasp. 'Gaetano knows this for certain?'

'He saw them many times outside the basilica at the Piazza del Popolo, though he never could place di Breme or Byron at one of his own Carbonari meetings – they all wore masks when they met in secret. It was dangerous for a man to reveal his identity in case any of them were arrested and tortured; if so, they could not expose anyone beyond their own close contacts. But in his everyday movements, Byron was less secretive.'

'As a British aristocrat, he had the protection of his wealth and position, even if he was conspiring against the Austrian government. And Byron never believed the laws applied to him,' I observed with some asperity.

A glint of dark humor crossed his face. 'Nevertheless, he was playing a dangerous game.'

And it all began during that summer of 1816 at the Villa Diodati in Geneva when Ludovico di Breme appeared and, shortly thereafter, someone pushed me down the stairs at nearby Castle Chillon. The three of them became bound together subsequently by some shadowy deception. Byron, di Breme, Polidori.

'Could it be that di Breme's appearance in Geneva all those years ago was by design?' I posed. 'By his account, he was visiting Madame de Stael and she had given him letters of introduction to our circle. But that could have been a ruse to meet Byron at the Villa Diodati and persuade him and Polidori to join the brotherhood.'

'The spirit of liberty always stirred Byron's finer feelings,' Trelawny observed, 'and an appeal from a fellow poet would have been even more enticing. Did you overhear anything . . . remarkable during his visit?'

'Not really – just a few snatches of conversation that may have touched on the *Risorgimento*, but nothing about joining a secret society of revolutionaries.' Closing my eyes briefly, I tried to re-summon more details about that beautiful day under the striped awning at the villa. The incessant rain had let up for the afternoon, and the sun had crept out from behind dark, heavy clouds. The soft summer air turned warm and balmy. A day of light and happiness. 'Mary and I were lounging on the portico with Shelley when Byron emerged from the villa with di Breme; they had been inside for a long time, and I assumed they had been talking about poetry. When they joined us, nothing seemed unusual – at first. Then, after I made his acquaintance, he seemed to be watching me very closely. I assumed it was because of the local gossip about Mary and me, but it made me uncomfortable. He could not stay for dinner but proposed that we meet later to chat. Then Byron quickly intervened and I never saw di Breme again. It was not long after that I had the supposedly "accidental" fall at Castle Chillon, and I forgot all about our Italian guest until Mr Rossetti gave Polidori's journal to me, and I spied his name again.' I paused. 'You told me that Byron connected my fall with di Breme's arrival, but that he never stated why he was so suspicious.'

'Either di Breme or someone with him may have wanted you out of the way so that nothing would prevent Byron from joining the Carbonari. Granted, Polidori was not working against you, yet his journal entries made it clear he and Mary had privately discussed Byron's "latest predicament" with di Breme, noting some kind of "grave consequences." A child changes a man's priorities,' Trelawny reflected as he crossed his legs and leaned back into the chair. 'Sadly, Mary never related that conversation to me.'

Nor me.

My famous stepsister had always been an intensely reserved person, shielding her inner thoughts from the outside world, and she kept this meeting a secret from me as well. 'She and Polidori both knew Shelley and I were making arrangements with Byron about my unborn child, so that could have been the "predicament" that Polidori referenced in his journal. Even if they did nothing more than share gossip with di Breme, she should have told me, especially after my suspicious fall at Chillon.'

Mary, I was always honest with you and loved you dearly as if you were my own blood relative. Why could you not have done the same for me?

Trelawny shifted his glance to his black leather boots, buffed to a high sheen. 'Mary chased her own demons, yet I find myself wishing she could have been more open with us about what drove her silence on this matter.'

'She was not one to indulge in idle chatter with people unfamiliar to her, so I cannot imagine what would have caused her to mention my . . . condition to di Breme. At best, indiscreet; at worst, a willful lie.' Then again, Mary's jealousy over my friendship with Shelley often caused her to act in petty ways that distressed me. A sarcastic comment said in my presence, or even a biting criticism overheard when she did not know I was nearby. Mary could be quite possessive over Shelley, always trying to shrink my role in their lives, especially after his death, as I had so recently found out from Mr Rossetti. 'You did not know?'

His jaw tightened as he looked up quickly. 'On my honor, I never spoke with her about di Breme. Beyond that, I cannot say what secrets Mary held from you; after Shelley died, I saw her only occasionally in England, and she had grown distant.'

Staring at him for several long moments, I amended my tone. 'I believe you. Exposing old wounds causes nothing beyond hard feelings. You came to Italy to tell me the truth, and even though it has come so late in my life, I will always be grateful for that knowledge, wherever it finally takes us.'

'I hope it leads to your dearest wish of finding Allegra.' Trelawny visibly relaxed into the chair again. 'No matter what transpired between Mary and di Breme, or how he saw your role in Byron's life, I now think it is possible he came to

Geneva to convince Byron of the justness of Italy's cause and to join the Carbonari. I had always assumed Teresa and Pietro converted him in Ravenna, but perhaps it occurred much earlier during the encounter with di Breme.'

Ludovico di Breme? *Il Gran Maestro?*

A sudden image rose up in my brain as I recalled the tableau of Shelley shaking hands with di Breme while I pretended to watch the sun glint on the lake's surface; as it did so, the light caught a reflection of the Italian's ring on his left hand. It flashed a thin, opaque beam on rose gold. Just an instant's vision.

Picking up the stickpin again, I held it up as if it were a talisman with the magic to bring that deeply buried memory into clear focus. But all things forgotten still lingered in some part of our minds. In that vein, I struggled to summon an image of di Breme as he appeared before us that day: a fashionable figure in striped trousers and a black, cut-away coat, his hair touching the collar, and jeweled ornaments on his cuffs and hands. 'I . . . I think di Breme wore a ring with a triangular emblem around some kind of object—'

'A hatchet?' he broke in eagerly.

Closing my eyes, I tried to envision the ring once more but, beyond its compass-like decorative seal, I could recall nothing else. With a murmur of dissent, I raised my lids. 'It was too brief a glimpse – barely a split second – before I looked away. Even if it had happened only a fortnight ago, I am not sure I would remember it clearly.'

The veil of old age has darkened my faculties over the years.

'But safe to say that *something* about it caught your attention,' Trelawny added.

'It was certainly not the typical man's signet ring.' I lowered the stickpin to my lap and covered it with my palm, careful not to prick myself. 'But that does not really prove anything other than that di Breme liked unusual jewelry. It is ironic that I did not notice more about him during his visit since it was out of the ordinary, but I was in love – totally preoccupied with Byron . . .'

'I know.' Trelawny touched my shoulder with a soft gesture of reassurance. 'I have no doubt that more details may occur to you now that you have kindled these long-lost thoughts. One tiny spark of memory can ignite a whole tinderbox of recollections. Just give yourself time.'

I gave a short laugh. 'That may be the one item in short supply.'

'On the contrary, your perceptions seem unusually sharp in spite of what you have endured these last few weeks, and we will see this through . . .' His voice lowered to a tender, throaty whisper that seemed to float over and surround me with its velvet warmth. It felt comforting to know, at long last, someone stood behind me with a strength of devotion and purpose.

A sweet promise.

'Thank you, Edward,' I said as I covered his hand with mine. 'Looking back can be maddening because so much was unclear to me then. If I had the insight that has come to me so recently, I would have behaved in such a different manner . . . maybe even enough to have not lost my daughter. But that is what Byron wanted, and who was I to contradict him? I was so young, and he was so famous that I hardly considered him a man at all, but rather a god. I cannot believe I was so unrealistic.'

'We all desire the wisdom of age in the season of youth, but wishing for that does nothing but cause sorrow and regret.' He gave my fingers one last squeeze before letting go. 'And in the end, you cannot know whether your actions would have changed anything about Allegra's fate. Besides, it appears that larger forces were at play than you fully realized. Much was hidden.'

'I suppose so.' I let Trelawny's words sink into my heart, knowing he spoke the truth. The past could never be altered. All I could do was take this new knowledge and move forward with a new awareness of what I could do in this time and place.

Only then could I fully forgive myself.

'You just mentioned "a quartet of conspirators." Who was the fourth man in Byron's little group? Did Gaetano know him?'

'Apparently.' Trelawny paused. 'The toymaker even thought he might have a drawing of him with the others hidden in his attic since he sketched scenes around Ravenna during that time.'

'Who was this man?'

'Gaetano would not tell me his name. When I pressed him, he grew more nervous at further unburdening his soul because he knows what is at stake. Though most of the Carbonari are now dead, they may have children and grand-children who want to keep the old secrets dead and buried. If not, vendettas can stretch across the generations.'

'They can indeed.' I flinched as something disturbing flickered behind Trelawny's eyes. 'All the cruel acts that have followed in the wake of Matteo's death must be connected with longstanding feuds; they have been stirred up once more, and my search for Allegra has been the catalyst. Unresolved conflicts cannot remain buried forever.'

'And if anyone knows who might be hiding in the dim alleyways of the past to settle old scores it is Gaetano, which makes his final words to me even more compelling.' Trelawny leaned forward and looked at me intently. 'He asked me to return for a late tea this evening and promised to reveal the identity of the fourth man . . . only to *you*.'

'Me?' I blinked in astonishment. 'But I am not even acquainted with him.'

'No, but he obviously has something to share about this man which has a connection to you . . . and Byron. But perhaps I am reading too much into his request.'

And Allegra? Setting my chin at an angle that granted no protest, I responded, 'We shall take him up on his invitation.'

'It may not be a good idea, but it seems as if we have no choice but to agree to his terms.' Trelawny tapped the sword holstered at his belt as if to say he would be prepared for any unexpected events. 'Be ready by six o'clock.'

I nodded.

The time of reckoning . . .

Trying not to obsess over the upcoming meeting with Gaetano, I spent the afternoon packing my things in the well-worn brown leather travel trunk – dresses, lingerie, and shawls – ready for our departure the next day. Heavy items on the bottom, then silk evening gowns, and, finally, cotton day attire layered in neat order. As I filled up the linen-lined interior, placing layers of tissue between the frocks, fleeting thoughts of Gaetano would drift through my mind, along with scattered images of his toyshop. Luckily, Paula and Georgiana kept popping into my room, diverting me with their excited chatter about being on the road again tomorrow.

'Aunt Claire, could you manage to find room for Georgiana's cup-and-ball toy?' Paula inquired as she strolled in for the third time, carrying the hand-carved plaything that I had purchased at Gaetano's. 'I cannot spend six hours in the carriage tomorrow with her rattling that ball in the cup . . . and we seem to have filled up her travel bag with new clothing and dolls.'

'It is *definitely* not the best toy for a long trip.' I took it from her and tucked it carefully between the dresses. 'Why is it travelers always leave with more than they brought with them?'

Paula laughed as she brushed back a stray blond curl. 'You never seem to have that problem.'

'A skill born of long experience, my dear.' I set a silver-gilt hand mirror atop the lace neckline of my favorite day dress. Looking down, I caught my reflection in the rippled glass and took in the slight loosening of skin around my jaw and tiny, feather-like lines radiating around my eyes.

Beauty's daughter grown old.

The blank canvas of youth had been painted over by every experience of my life: faint shadows in the hollows of my cheeks and a bit of a droop around the mouth. Every experience had caused a brushstroke that altered the image I had once seen in this mirror – some of it good and some of it bad – but I did not really care, so long as I did not lose that ability to embrace the shifts of time. Turning the mirror over to protect the glass, I covered it with another piece of tissue. 'My many journeys have helped me to perfect the art of travel. I suppose that is one of the benefits of not staying in the same place too long.'

London, Geneva, Paris, Moscow – all cities I have lived in but never really called home.

Only Florence stirred a deep sense of connectedness inside of me.

La mia casa.

My home.

'At least you did not have the chance to grow bored and tired in the same familiar surroundings.' In spite of her cavalier words, Paula's voice turned wistful as she sat on the bed and fingered the copper rivets on my trunk. Unlike me, she had come to Italy *because* she wanted a fixed and stable place to raise Georgiana; I could not blame her. My own restless nature might have been tamed if Allegra had remained with me, and I was occupied with the responsibilities of motherhood.

'There is also a kind of peace that comes from being rooted in the same soil,' I added as I shook out my gauzy, fringed shawl and laid it flat next to the trunk, ready to wear in the morning when we left. 'It provides comfort as the world keeps spinning every faster.'

Paula propped up her elbows behind her and leaned back. 'I am surprised to hear you speak so. Is it possible that my adventurous aunt is finally ready to cease her vagabond days?'

'All good things must come to an end, and I have seen more than enough of the world to spend my final days in contentment at the Palazzo Cruciato apartment. In fact, after the last few weeks, it will be a relief to have our lives settle into an ordinary routine again. No matter how this matter of Allegra's fate turns out, I want to see you and Georgiana secure with some of the money the Cades sketch will fetch.' I threaded my fingers through the shawl's fringe, smoothing out the tangles and knots. 'There is nothing I want more than to know if my daughter is still alive . . . except to know that you will not face poverty again.'

'Oh, Aunt Claire.' Paula's voice broke as tears welled up in her eyes. 'You are too good to me.'

'It is only what you deserve,' I said gently, touching her cheek for a brief instant. 'I know we have not always agreed in the past – we are two strong-willed women – and that caused friction between us, but you and Georgiana have transformed my life. There is nothing that I would not do to ensure your happiness.'

Her face brightened like the long-stemmed Italian sunflowers opening their petals at dawn. 'I am beyond grateful . . . and I know Raphael also appreciates your generosity, as well. He admires you so much for giving him a chance to prove his worth when no one else would hire him.'

The moment's luster dimmed slightly when she spoke his name.

Raphael.

I turned away to retrieve a pile of freshly laundered handkerchiefs. 'He has certainly been a constant . . . companion on our trip, and I hope he will continue to be after we return to Florence.' The words sounded stilted even to me, and I could feel Paula's curiosity stir behind me as I pretended to focus on stacking the cotton squares in a uniform bundle. When I finished, I sorted through the trunk's contents to find a place for them, keeping my attention downward.

'Are you questioning Raphael's fidelity?' she queried, snatching the handkerchiefs from me. 'He has been with us every step of the way, unwavering in his pledge to protect Georgiana and me, even risking his life when Matteo threatened to kill us. Why would you doubt him now, just when we might be able to build a life together?'

Raphael's surprising declaration in the carriage ride through the woods of Filetto drifted back through my mind: *I must find my own way to support Paula and Georgiana. Anything less would be deemed dishonorable behavior.* He said he loved my niece but could not marry her. Yet he remained in her life, continuing on with their affair and pledging to be a part of my search for Allegra. Did he stay because of his affection for Paula or his desire to continue the plotting that his boss, Matteo, had begun?

My eyes caught and held hers, but I said nothing.

Paula threw the handkerchiefs aside and rose swiftly to her feet. 'I do not understand your sudden change of heart over Raphael. I love him – truly and deeply – and I cannot imagine my life without him. He may not have an aristocratic pedigree, but he is more of a gentleman than any man I have ever met, including Georgiana's feckless father,' she declared passionately. 'Is that the problem? Raphael is not respectable enough?'

'Of course not,' I bristled. 'Do you really think I, of all people, would believe *that* when I do not even know the identity of my own father?'

'No,' she admitted grudgingly. 'Then why are you expressing qualms about his character?'

Tell her . . . everything.

'I . . . I have no misgivings about him.' Every fiber in my body screamed out in protest at the lie, but I could not bring myself to relate what Raphael had told me – and his reluctance to marry her, even if I did bestow a small financial settlement on her. It would crush her as surely as if I had taken a vice and squeezed the life out of her hopes and dreams, leaving only the empty void of bitterness and sorrow. I could not do it. 'I simply meant that he may not want to travel on with us after our stop in Florence because of any pressing tasks that need to be done at the palazzo apartments.'

Paula exhaled in a long sigh. 'I had not thought of that . . . as the *tuttofare*, Raphael will need to see to the other tenants. Especially now that Matteo is gone, there is no one to oversee the residence until his aunt takes over. I hope she will look favorably on Raphael, perhaps even elevate him to *direttore*.'

'He certainly deserves it after his years of steady work for Matteo.' As I spoke, a sudden thought occurred to me: if Raphael took on this new status at the Palazzo Cruciato, he could not make any more excuses not to marry Paula on his own merits. At that point, his true intentions toward her would be revealed. I would also know by then if Baldini had found anything dubious in his background.

'Oh, yes.' She clapped her hands. 'I would gladly sacrifice having him accompany us to Livorno if it meant he could raise his station in life from a laborer; it would open the world to him.'

My mouth turned up a notch – not quite a smile – as I struggled with my uncertainty. I could only pray that my fears were unfounded and that Paula's lover was simply a proud man who wanted to stand beside her as an equal.

Just then, I heard rapid steps clattering along the outside hallway, and Georgiana burst into the room. *'Zia Claire!'*

'Dolcezza mia.' I flung out my arms, and she barreled ahead,

burying herself in the folds of my skirt. 'Are you excited that we are returning home tomorrow? You will be able to see your friend, Maria, and not be confined in a stuffy hotel all day. It will be a welcome relief, will it not?'

'*Sì, Zia.*' She pulled back and gazed up at me, her eyes wide and pleading. 'But Mama said I could not bring my toy in the carriage because it makes too much noise. Please ask her to let me have it. I will be quiet.'

'Your mama has the final word on this matter,' I told her gently. 'But I am going to the toymaker's shop before dinner, and I shall find you something that does not create such a clamor. Perhaps a little puzzle?'

Georgiana's shoulders drooped.

'That would be lovely,' Paula enthused as she reached for the handkerchiefs and covered over the cup and ball nestled in my trunk. 'Say thank you.'

But Georgiana would have none of it. She flounced out of the room before I could protest.

Paula turned to me with a helpless little shrug. 'There is no need to make a special stop; Georgiana has plenty of dolls and books to occupy her on the road. And I am hoping to tire her out so she will sleep most of the way back to Florence tomorrow.'

'Not likely.' I raised one brow in amusement. 'And it is hardly an inconvenience to see the toymaker again since his shop is just off the Via Cavour. Perhaps Signora Elisa will have your dresses finished, as well, so I can take care of both tasks at the same time.' As she gave me a brief hug in response, I felt a twinge of guilt over not telling her the real reason I was visiting Gaetano's shop. But if I did so, I would have to explain how Trelawny came to meet him – *and* how we found the stickpin in the dead fox, and how we suspected someone connected to the Carbonari might be behind the vicious acts against us.

A cascade of omissions unfolding into one big deception – the very thing that had so angered me about Trelawny's keeping secrets from me.

But lying to protect Paula was not exactly the same, was it?

'I had better rein in Georgiana before she gets into any

further mischief,' Paula groaned, heading quickly for the door. 'That child will drive me to Bedlam.'

Once she had exited, I slumped on to the bed and closed my eyes, trying to blot out what I had just done. But it was impossible. I saw only too clearly the truth of my sham pretenses and knew I would be called upon eventually to confess and ask for my niece's forgiveness. For now, I could only hope and pray that once Raphael's real motive was revealed, he would not disappoint Paula.

Byron once said that 'truth is a gem that is found at a great depth,' and, in this instance, I wanted it to be the priceless jewel of true love.

A treasured delight.

And I anticipated that our visit to Gaetano's shop would be no less positive. Perhaps even illuminative.

At that optimistic thought, my eyelids fluttered open, and I scanned the last vestiges of what remained to be packed: my linen nightgown and matching jacket which I would wear tonight. A pair of slippers. Some assorted toiletries.

Otherwise, I was finished . . .

The church bells began to ring from the brick tower of the Basilica di San Vitale – five chimes that signified an hour to go until Trelawny and I left for Gaetano's. Rising, I moved to the window and threw it open, perching on the velvet seat as I watched the nearly deserted street below. Breathing in the warm late-afternoon air, I spied only two young boys running along with a rolling hoop as they passed an elderly man hobbling along with a fluffy, white-haired dog. Young and old, passing each other as if they did not exist. Caught up in their own generation's activities where the worlds rarely collided, they lived with the present as it moved into the past, but no one cared to record the moment – except those who sensed the import of what was occurring.

Like Pietro.

Slowly swiveling my head, I focused on Pietro's correspondence again.

As a young man drawn into Byron's orbit, he somehow knew their shared adventures would become almost mythical; fortunately for me, he wrote about them to Teresa, which gave me a window into those moments in Byron's life that I had never seen.

Days of dreams and revolution.

Sailing into eternity.

Strolling away from the window, I picked up my spectacles and made myself comfortable on the settee again with Pietro's letters in hand . . .

At Argostoli, Cephalonia, aboard the Hercules
August 1823

My dearest Teresa,

We have been docked at Argostoli for over a week – a pretty harbor on the west coast of Cephalonia that looks somewhat like Venice. But Byron will not allow us to disembark because our situation is tenuous. Our mission to coordinate the naval fleet for the Greeks to take back their country has not yet been sanctioned by the English powers who rule this island.

Day after day, I stare at the jagged coastline of pastel-colored villas along the shoreline and then, further behind, into the mountainous terrain dotted with fir and pine trees. I long to feel the earth beneath my feet again as I imagine myself rambling through the streets and open piazzas. Yet we remain confined on the Hercules, *on the edge of the war.*

So close to the next battlefield, yet stuck in this limbo of inaction because everything is at a standstill.

The different factions are still arguing among themselves from established positions already in Greece as to how to proceed with a full invasion, and Byron does not want to go ashore lest he be seen showing allegiance to their emissaries on one side or the other. He meets with the British governor, Colonel Napier, almost daily, trying to find a way to convene all of the Greek leaders in one place at Argostoli. Sadly, it seems nearly impossible. They are all clamoring for the money that Byron has brought with him but not willing to work together to use it to unify their troops and defeat the Turkish oppressors.

Alas, there is no one willing to come forward and compromise.

A small boat brought us supplies yesterday from the town, which likely means this impasse will linger on and on.

So, we wait . . .

I noticed Captain Vitalis has also remained on board, though he could easily have left the ship and made his way home to Greece. Curiously, he has given no sign of being ready to depart. I am watching him even more carefully now since he inserts himself into every conversation that Byron has with Napier, offering 'advice' on how to deal with his fellow Greek countrymen. But there is something shifty in his constant attempts to make himself indispensable; he is too forward, too self-serving.

When I mentioned my concerns again to Byron, he said Vitalis might provide some assistance to us, but his frown told me he, too, was concerned about the true purpose of the man's lingering presence. Mercenaries lurk everywhere, and it is difficult to tell an ally from an adversary . . .

Byron tries to be cheerful about the confusion and chaos but, yesterday, he despaired to me: Dopo mesi di lavoro siamo giunti a un punto morto – *after all of our work, we have a stalemate.*

Still, we carry on.

To divert myself, I sea-bathe in the mornings and practice my fencing in the afternoons with Vitalis's companion, Gaetano, who befriended me on the voyage. Much taller than I, with a long reach, he is a formidable opponent. He is also teaching me how to carve toys from wood. Even though I have not learned to master the whittling knife, we have become friends since I learned he is from Ravenna—

I jerked up my head.

Could this Gaetano be the toymaker whom Trelawny and I had just met? How many men with that name harkened from

Ravenna and carved wooden toys? His age would be right, as would Pietro's description of his skill as a carver. And Trelawny did say he had looked somewhat familiar.

Quickly, I scanned Pietro's letter again and then sat back in dazed wonderment. If Gaetano were, indeed, the same man whom Pietro mentioned, it opened up all sorts of questions. Was his presence aboard the *Hercules* somehow connected with his Carbonari activities? Why did he want to befriend Pietro? Who was Captain Vitalis, and how did he happen to accompany this young man from Ravenna on his way to Greece?

My thoughts began to tumble with unbridled abandon, going back and forth between different possibilities, barely registering one before moving on to another. First, Gaetano appeared as an evil rogue aligned with Vitalis for some nefarious purpose; then he shifted back to an innocent young man, caught up in events beyond his awareness. Or perhaps a little of both?

Removing my spectacles, I covered my eyes with my hands, trying to quell all of these conflicting images. I was so desperately trying to reason things out when, in the end, they might all mean nothing more than a series of haphazard links to the past. Yet I could not deny that Gaetano had revealed secrets to Trelawny that could place him at risk.

Perhaps I was going mad . . .

A firm knock at the door startled me back to the present.

Still grasping the letter, I rushed to answer it as I reached for my shawl. 'Trelawny, we must leave now for Gaetano's shop. I have discovered something that seems to shed new light on our Ravenna toymaker; *he* could have been involved in a conspiracy connected to Byron far beyond the Carbonari.'

'That affable carver?' he queried in disbelief.

'Trust me, we cannot delay . . . he might hold the key to more than the stickpin.' I pushed Trelawny out of the door as I handed him Pietro's letter. 'When you read this note, you will understand what I mean.'

Descending the stairs, we strolled through the lobby with a brief wave at the manager. As we emerged on to the street, we passed the fruit seller who was taking in his crates of leftover produce. He tipped his hat and handed me a ripe peach, and I thanked him as I slipped it into my bag. Townspeople were emerging from their homes for the *la passeggiata* – the evening stroll – and we gave the customary greeting but did not pause for long.

Trelawny attempted to read the letter as we headed toward the Via Cavour; in his distraction, he bumped into a young man, almost knocking him down. The youth spat out a curse in Italian even as Trelawny tried to apologize profusely. But he would have none of it and stalked off, muttering *anziano* – old man – along with a rude hand gesture.

'I cannot concentrate on it.' Trelawny folded the letter and placed it in his jacket pocket. 'What did Pietro say?'

'Remember when you mentioned that Gaetano looked familiar?' I queried, linking my arm in his while I negotiated the uneven, cobblestoned street. 'In spite of his failing eyesight, I have no doubt that *he* recognized you.'

'I do not understand.'

We turned the corner at the Via Gamba and I stopped him in front of Gaetano's storefront. Placing a hand against Trelawny's chest, I tilted my head up and squinted in the afternoon sunlight as I took in his puzzled expression. 'Do you remember that Captain Vitalis brought a travel companion with him when he boarded the *Hercules*?'

'Vaguely . . . I was occupied with our ship's supplies and monitoring our route, so I barely noticed him.'

'Luckily, Pietro befriended him while you were docked at the harbor in Cephalonia and learned that he was a toymaker from Ravenna named Gaetano. They became constant companions, so you would have seen them together.' I watched the light of realization dawn in Trelawny's eyes. 'Do you recall him now?'

'Damn it all.' Taking a quick look at the sign above the shop, Trelawny gave a grunt of recognition. 'He and Vitalis remained with us when we disembarked for our stay at Argostoli, but I had little conversation with him. I never even learned his name.'

'But he, no doubt, recognized *your* name when you contacted him this morning. Afterwards, he probably made inquiries and found out why we had traveled here, though it does not explain why he wanted to see *me* specifically,' I pointed out, then I took a deep breath. 'I expect we are about to learn why.'

We remained motionless for a few moments, then Trelawny pushed open the door, and we moved inside. A silent interior greeted us, and the woodsy, cedar smell wafted over me once again with its pungent odor. After my vision adjusted to the dim light, I spied Signora Elisa standing in the back of the room, her head down. I called out a greeting, but she did not look up. As we approached, I saw what lay at her feet.

Gaetano was sprawled on the floor, his head at an odd angle and eyes wide with a glassy stare.

He was dead.

Convent of San Giovanni, Bagnacavallo, Italy
Christmas Eve 1821

Allegra's story . . .

I have given up all hope of ever seeing Papa again. It has been months since he last visited, and I received only one letter from him: a short note to say he now resided at the Palazzo Lanfranchi in Pisa and would send for me as soon as possible.

But I had heard those promises from him before.

And nothing happened.

Every day in December, I went to morning Mass and prayed to the Madonna that I might join Papa for Christmas, but my appeals went unanswered. Even so, I would sometimes slip into the abbess's office and look up at *Madre Maria's* portrait, beseeching her to persuade Papa to bring me home, but her image simply gazed down at me with a blank look.

I was all alone.

As I walked through the convent's hallways so late this evening, my footsteps echoed through the empty spaces. An empty sound. I stopped in front of the small chapel where the other girls and I would begin our day with morning prayers, but all of them had left to spend the holiday with their families. I had only Sister Anna. I think she felt sorry for me because she had moved my belongings temporarily into her rooms and would make my favorite *pasta e fagioli* soup in the evenings. We would then read the Bible together until I drifted off to sleep, dreaming of my days in Ravenna when life was so happy.

It was *la vigilia di Natale* – Christmas Eve – but I did not expect Papa to send for me, unless a miracle happened.

And I did not believe in miracles anymore.

I felt a soft hand on my shoulder, and I looked up to see Sister Anna smiling down at me.

'It is almost time for Midnight Mass, so shall we place one last figure in the nativity scene?' She held up a tiny terracotta angel and pointed at the *presepe* near the altar.

Nodding, I took it from her and moved toward the front of the church, halting near the crib that Sister Anna and I set up two weeks ago. Carefully reaching in, I positioned the angel behind the figures of Joseph and Mary. Then I spread the thin layer of straw around the Holy Family, so it looked like the stable floor at *la Nascita di Gesu* – the birth of Jesus.

Gloria Patri.

'St Francis would be proud of your *presepe*,' Sister Anna murmured as she stood behind me. 'Way back in the thirteenth century, he had the first nativity scene created in an old cave near Greccio to honor our Savior, and we have been putting them up ever since, so you are sharing in a wonderous tradition.'

'I suppose so.' Feeling my throat closing up, I turned away from the nativity scene. 'It makes me want to be with my own papa.'

Sister Anna hugged me. 'Do not despair, *Allegrina*, for your papa loves you dearly and would have you with him if it were possible. In the meantime, *we* will be your family. The abbess is going to have a dinner for those of us still at the convent, and we will feast together on seafood and *panettone*, then sing hymns for the salvation of our souls. Trust me, you will not be disappointed. There is still much joy in the world.'

Not for me.

Slowly, she released me but kept her hand on my shoulder as she straightened the small linen square that covered Jesus in his cradle. Tucking in the corners around the baby figure, Sister Anna hummed, then abruptly stopped and leaned forward. Instantly, she pulled back and tried to push me behind her.

But I caught a glimpse of what she had seen: the figure's painted eyes had fallen out.

Un cattivo auspicio – a bad omen.

'Do you see that, Sister Anna? The baby Jesus has no eyes.'

'It is just an old *statuetta* which is crumbling apart.' She plucked it out of the cradle and shoved it in her dress pocket. 'We will replace it with a new one.'

Her voice sounded shaky, and her mouth trembled.

She was scared.

SEVEN

'I saw thee weep – the big bright tear
Came o'er that eye of blue . . .'

Byron, 'I Saw Thee Weep,' 1–2

Ravenna, Italy
July 1873

I could not take my glance off the horrific sight of Gaetano's body, limp and lifeless. As long as I lived on this earth, I would never grow used to seeing what remained after the spirit's departure to heaven – just a vacant, empty shell. Only yesterday, I saw him bent over his bench, intently occupied with carving a piece of cherry wood into a toy. Only yesterday, I marveled at his skill with the hammer and chisel. Only yesterday, I expressed my gratitude for his kindness. And now he was gone.

Crossing myself, I murmured a prayer for the salvation of his soul.

Trelawny knelt and brushed his fingers over Gaetano's face to shut his eyes. 'Signora, what happened?' he inquired softly.

She made a choking sound as the tears streamed down her cheeks. 'When I came in a few minutes ago, I found him here. He had sent me a note to say that he was going to have tea with English visitors at his shop and wanted to talk with me first – urgently. So I closed up and came rushing over.' Visibly shaking, she covered her heart, digging her fingers into the bodice of her dress. '*Il mio povero marito.*'

Her poor husband.

Reaching out to Elisa, I grasped her hand, which felt icy cold. 'I am so sorry that you have lost him.'

She wept quietly, biting her lower lip so hard that the skin turned red. Then she moved over to one of the shelves and jerked the velvet cloth from underneath a toy horse and wagon set with a violent motion; the wooden trinkets spilled out on to the floor, snapping apart as they hit the hard stones. After staring at the broken pieces for a few moments, she took in a deep breath and passed the material to Trelawny who covered Gaetano's body with it.

We all remained rooted in place and mute until Trelawny slowly rose to his feet again.

'Did you send for a doctor, Signora?' He skirted around Gaetano's body, careful not to step on a broken toy, and retrieved a broom from a hook on the wall.

'*Sì.*' She slid on to a nearby chair. '*Il Dottore Murano.* He attended to my husband for many years.'

'Was he ill?' I asked.

She dabbed at her eyes with a handkerchief, then crumpled it into a ball. 'I noticed that he would become short of breath when we walked to the piazza in the evenings. He said it was nothing, but I noticed *il dottore* came by the house more frequently and would check his heart. They would whisper between themselves, just out of my hearing, so I suspected that Gaetano was not telling me the whole truth. He was a proud and strong man.'

'Then, it might be likely that he had a . . . heart attack?' Lowering my voice to a whisper, I tried not to say anything that would upset her further. Trelawny said nothing as he swept the wooden fragments into a corner, but I could sense he was carefully listening.

She shrugged. '*È difficile da dire.*'

'The doctor should be able to tell if that is what happened,' Trelawny said as he finished his task and rehung the broom on its hook. 'Would you like to rest upstairs with Claire until he arrives? I can stay with Gaetano.'

'No, I shall remain.' Her face settled into resolute lines. 'I was with him for fifty years in life and will not desert him in death.'

We did not have to wait long before a middle-aged man wearing spectacles and carrying a small, black bag came rushing through the door. He introduced himself and we did the same before he quickly made his way to Gaetano's inert form. Hesitating for a second, Dr Murano leaned down, pulled back the sheet, and checked for a pulse on the wrist, then the neck. After listening to his chest with a stethoscope, the doctor shook his head.

Elisa began to weep again, rocking back and forth. I moved closer and slipped an arm around her shoulder, allowing her to cry until she eventually quieted and pulled back with a lost and dazed expression. 'I know I probably should have been reconciled to Gaetano's ill health, but he did not seem sick enough for his heart to simply give out so suddenly . . .'

'Is that what you think happened, *Dottore*?' Trelawny inquired.

As he straightened again, Dr Murano coiled up the stethoscope and dropped it into his bag, then adjusted his spectacles. 'Gaetano had a weak heart and was certainly showing signs of fatigue, yet . . . he had been fairly stable for the last six months. Hardly at the point of death. But these things cannot always be predicted with total accuracy.'

'Of course,' she replied. '*Grazie, Dottore.*'

As he gestured her off to the side, their conversation in Italian switched to the practical details that had to be addressed: death certificates and burial arrangements. I admired her ability to master her feelings enough to focus on these matters for I knew only too well how traumatic it was to rein in the raw grief when a beloved one was ripped from life so unceremoniously.

Almost unbearable.

Trelawny cleared his throat lightly, catching my attention, as he aimed his eyes downward. Puzzled, I followed his fixed stare on Gaetano's hand, partially visible from under the velvet cover, and noted his wrinkled fingers curled around a small piece of paper. During the initial discovery of this grim scene, I had missed it. Trelawny reached down, seemingly to adjust the velvet cover even as he took the paper from him in one, smooth motion. Pocketing it, he strolled over to one of the toy shelves and turned his back to us.

'Would you both mind staying here for a little longer?' the doctor asked as he assisted Elisa to be seated on the chair again; her tears had stopped, replaced by the vacant expression of a lost child. 'It will take a little time to have someone remove Gaetano's . . . body, and I do not want her to be alone.'

'Of course,' I agreed readily.

'*Dottore*, I know you might be reluctant to state that he died of a heart attack, but would that be your best guess considering what you just said about his weak heart?' Trelawny swiveled back in our direction. 'I am curious because I met with him only this morning, and he seemed well.'

'Unfortunately, as I said, the heart can be unstable, and Gaetano's particularly so. He could go for weeks without any symptoms, then find himself in discomfort with chest pains – and these episodes had grown more severe recently.' The doctor removed his spectacles and rubbed his temples before replacing them again. 'Given his age and history, I would say it is very likely that is what happened.'

'I see,' Trelawny said in a neutral tone.

'The only thing that I find out of the ordinary is that his fingers are not blue,' the doctor added with a frown. 'Most times, a heart attack will starve oxygen from the extremities, which causes the skin color to change, but that did not happen to Gaetano. His hands looked normal. Then again, if death came swiftly, he might not have struggled to breathe, which would explain it.' He shrugged. 'In truth, I cannot say for certain what killed him.'

Or whom?

Unbidden, those two words floated through my mind. Considering Gaetano's urgent message to his wife before our arrival and the physician's uncertainty about his last moments, I found myself wondering if he did, indeed, die of natural causes. It seemed likely from the doctor's explanation, but, then again, if Gaetano had been preparing to reveal to us the hidden identity of Byron's Carbonari ally, his demise certainly had suspicious timing.

I sensed from Trelawny's continued scrutiny of the body that he, too, had doubts about the cause of death. Drawing closer to the doctor, I heard him whisper, 'Gaetano seems to have fallen backwards, but would he not land face down if he had heart failure? As a soldier, I have seen many men die

during my lifetime – both from natural and unnatural causes
– and his body position suggests the latter.'

Dr Murano took a brief glance at Elisa before answering
in a low murmur, 'I do not mean to doubt your expertise,
Signor, but if you are suggesting that Gaetano was murdered,
I would have to disagree. He was a generous man, loved by
one and all in Ravenna; he had many friends and few enemies
– certainly no one who wished him dead. I would have to ask
that you do not upset the signora with such talk . . . this
situation is difficult enough without adding to her grief with
baseless speculations.'

'Hardly that.' Trelawny stiffened. 'If violence has been done
to him, you should want to find the truth and bring the killer
to account. Anything less would be an even worse crime.'

The doctor snapped his bag shut. 'Even if what you say is
true, I have no way to prove that Gaetano did not die from a
heart attack. And if we call the *polizia*, they will take state-
ments, ask questions, then close the case, since there is no
evidence to prove it one way or the other – and the signora
will always have doubts about how her beloved husband died.
Please do not meddle in affairs that do not concern you. I am
the one who completes the death certificate, and it will state
"natural causes." And you may rest assured that we take care
of our own in Ravenna.'

'Is that justice?'

'For us – *sì*.'

Trelawny muttered something under his breath but let the
matter drop as the doctor took his leave, promising that the
undertaker would arrive soon to take care of Gaetano.
Without a backward glance at us, he exited.

'I find it infuriating that the doctor did not even want to
pursue a line of inquiry about Gaetano's death,' Trelawny
speculated.

'Should *we* contact the police?'

'I do not think it would do any good since the doctor has
already said he will certify "natural causes," but I remain uncon-
vinced. Gaetano was going to reveal the name of an important
member of Byron's Carbonari network, information that
someone may not have wanted us to know . . . though I do have

this.' He reached into his pocket and pulled out a small, folded square of yellowed paper.

'What is that?' Elisa chimed in from the other side of the room; she could not hear what we were saying, but she had spied the document.

'Your husband told me this morning that he had a drawing he wanted to give me of . . . old friends. I found it just now next to him, so I assumed it was for me.' Trelawny opened the note, then he walked over to Elisa.

'He had the soul of an artist.' After Elisa took it from him, she laid it on her lap and smoothed out the curling corners. 'Aside from his woodworking, he loved to draw from the time he was a young man, mostly little mementos of people he knew or places he visited. Things he did not want to forget.'

I joined them and took in the simple pen-and-ink sketch of four male figures seated at a table. 'Do you . . . know them?' My eyes lingered on the undeniable likeness of Byron in the center of the group, his head slightly averted in the direction of the basilica behind him.

She nodded. 'Gaetano did this piece long ago, but I remember him showing it to me proudly because it included the poet, Lord Byron. He had spotted the poet in the piazza with the other three. It was during the dark days of the revolution, so he never shared it with anyone else because it was an open secret that they were all involved with the Carbonari.' She pointed at each figure, one by one, naming Byron, di Breme, and Polidori; on the last man, she hesitated because his face was turned aside. 'I . . . I cannot be sure.'

I scanned the roughly drawn portrait of a young man – slim with unruly hair flowing to his collar. Unfortunately, the sketch's pen strokes gave no details of his facial features.

'Would you mind if I kept it?' Trelawny proposed. 'I would certainly pay.'

She handed it to him. 'It is a gift from Gaetano and me.'

Now, tears stung at my eyes at her generosity. 'Once the undertaker arrives, is there someone who will be with you? Do you have a daughter or son?'

'I have a sister who the doctor has already sent for; other-wise, I have no one else since Gaetano and I did not have any children.' The smile faded as she bent her head again. 'It was a source of some pain for us that I could not conceive, especially when neither of his brothers had any *bambini* either – one was a priest and the other died fairly young. Gaetano was the last of his line, and now he is dead.'

'How sad,' I replied. 'Is it possible your priest brother-in-law can come to provide spiritual comfort for you?'

She heaved an audible sigh. 'He died not long ago, the victim of a horrible attack inside his own basilica in *Firenze*. When Gaetano heard the news, he was quite shaken . . . that may have further weakened his heart.'

Instantly, my pulse quickened. 'What was his brother's name?'

'You may have known him: Gianni Costa.' She paused and glanced at the drawing again. 'In fact, I think from the outlines of the figure in the sketch, he might be the fourth man in the group; he had that build and wild hair.'

Father Gianni?

Is that what Gaetano wanted to tell me? That my dear confessor was his brother – and known to Byron?

I merely stared, tongue-tied.

'He was a truly religious man, and their other brother, Stefano, was in the service of the great poet, Ludovico di Breme,' she added with a touch of awe in her voice. 'But they were all members of the Carbonari.' She pointed at the embroidered compass on the white silk curtain toward the back of the store; I had noted it on my first visit but missed the small hatchet symbol stitched next to it.

My God.

Stefano. Gianni. Gaetano.

The three brothers, all tied together as secret revolutionaries.

All at once, the room seem to convulse and narrow as if the universe were compressing the space, and I reached out to brace myself against one of the shelves. Trelawny moved swiftly to steady me, and I clutched his jacket while I tried to regain my balance.

'I . . . I was acquainted with Father Gianni.' I stared down at Gaetano, and the image of my beloved priest's broken body, lying at the base of the Medici statue in his church, materialized as a glossy specter over his brother's inert form. So similar in their position as they died. I shuddered. 'We all mourned his sudden and violent demise – just tragic.'

And I did mourn him, even if he took secrets to the grave that could have helped me in my search for Allegra.

'What happened to Stefano after di Breme passed away?' Trelawny queried, flashing a sidelong glance at me over Elisa's bowed head. 'Did he remain in Ravenna?'

'For a short time, but he was always a firebrand, restlessly aligning himself to different political causes, moving around Italy every time a new conflict broke out. When our fight for freedom turned hopeless, he then joined the Greek rebels, and that was the last time we ever heard from him. We assumed he died in a battle. I know Gaetano fretted over him during that time; he even secured a passage with Lord Byron when he sailed for Greece to find Stefano, but to no avail.'

Trelawny grasped her shoulder briefly. 'You should know I was on the *Hercules* with Gaetano, but it was so long ago that I did not immediately recognize him this morning. He had come aboard with a Greek named Vitalis and, then, kept to himself . . . with Pietro Gamba. And in Pietro's letters, he remembers your husband fondly. Gaetano asked me to return with Signora Clairmont because he had something to tell us about that time.'

Elisa shrugged. 'I do not remember his mentioning either man, only that he had been lucky enough to sail with Byron on his way to Greece.'

I struggled to take in the import of her words. 'So Gaetano sailed with Byron to find his brother – not to fight?'

'If he did, he kept those secrets to himself.' She shook her head. 'He spoke only occasionally of Lord Byron's role in liberating Greece, but always with awe and admiration. As a famous English lord who had proven himself by risking his life with the other Carbonari, he may have also inspired Gaetano to the Greek cause.'

How Byron would have loved to hear that kind of praise of himself as a leader of men in pursuit of liberty.

Self-sacrificing and noble.

As I had come to learn in the last few weeks, Italy had changed Byron in ways I did not understand at the time, being so preoccupied with fighting him for custody of Allegra. The erratic, capricious Albe of that 1816 summer in Geneva, when he had left England in disgrace and was desperately unhappy, had begun his transformation into a serious revolutionary. It did not completely excuse his behavior but it did take away some of the hurt.

'Gaetano must have been an admirable man as well.' Cold comfort, but it was all I could really offer to her at this point considering the suspicious nature of his death. Still, my heart went out to Elisa, knowing that she was dazed with the shock of discovering her husband's body and, in the weeks to come, grief would set in like a cold freeze before a distant spring. 'He will, no doubt, be missed greatly by everyone in Ravenna.'

'*Sì.*' One word. Nothing more needed to be spoken.

Just then, the front door swung open and a woman who bore a strong resemblance to Elisa rushed in, her arms stretched wide. Elisa cried out, '*Mia sorella!*' before rushing into her embrace. Her sister. They wept together, holding on to each other, as Elisa tried to explain in broken fragments what had occurred. But, after a few attempts, she gave up and simply rested her head on her sister's shoulder.

As my own eyes began to tear up again, I sensed that Trelawny wanted us to take our leave. He folded the drawing and placed it in his jacket pocket as I bid farewell to Elisa.

'Wait, Signora,' she said, reaching for a packet on the counter. 'I finished repairing your dresses.' She waved aside my attempt to pay her, then let her sister lead her through the back curtain.

Afterward, I took one last look around the shop at the pieces that Gaetano had lovingly carved and placed on the shelves. Tiny soldiers in painted uniforms standing to attention. Dollhouses decorated with pocket-sized furniture. Miniature horse-drawn carriages. They would disappear one by one, and the empty shelves would gradually gather layers of dust.

'He brought many children happiness with his toys, Claire,' Trelawny said, seemingly reading my melancholy thoughts, 'including Georgiana.'

Just hearing her name raised my spirits. 'A priceless legacy.'

As the undertaker's carriage drew up, Trelawny turned the shop sign on the door to *Chiuso. Closed – forever.* Then, we let ourselves out and, arm in arm, slowly strolled along the lane. *La passeggiata* had ended and the streets were mostly deserted, with only a few children straggling along the avenue, laughing together as they made their way home. Their joyful enthusiasm seemed jarring after the last few hours.

'If we could stop somewhere, I need to take a few moments to make sense of everything that we just heard,' I said, drawing Trelawny closer to me as we navigated the narrow sidewalk. 'I hardly know what to make of Gaetano's death, much less the labyrinth of lies that Father Gianni hid from me. And what do I tell Paula? In all of the turmoil, I completely forgot to pick up a toy puzzle for Georgiana.'

'That is the least of our problems.' He halted at the corner and looked up and down the Via Barbiani. 'I think there is a small church just a short walk from here; maybe we can sit in its garden for a little while and discuss our . . . options.'

'Perfect.'

As I let Trelawny lead the way, I still felt a bit off balance and kept a tight grip on his arm. He felt like the one solid, reliable presence in my world right now, when reality kept moving and shifting into unknown realms. The living died unexpectedly, and the dead refused to remain in the past – all at a breathless pace. But I was determined to keep moving forward.

In scarcely a quarter-hour, we reached an iron gate with a small sign:

Chiesa di Santa Eufemia
1742–1745
Arch Gianfrancesco Buonamici

'Saint Eufemia, the young girl who refused to commit pagan sacrifice and was burned at the stake,' I commented, taking in the small white-and-yellow stone building as Trelawny pushed open the gate. The *chiesa* held none of the magnificence of San Vitale or Sant'Apollinare, but its deserted garden held a profusion of lush flowers circled around a marble fountain that beckoned with its soothing, rhythmic water flow, streaming like soft whispers in the night air. 'Not exactly a happy legend but inspiring in some ways.'

A garden of roses and thorns.

'It honors the power of a woman's conviction.' He escorted

me toward a wooden bench positioned under the shade of an oak tree. 'I never underestimate it.'

Seating myself, I could not resist adding, 'But she was tortured and executed.'

'And, later, declared a saint.' He took his place beside me.

'Ah, yes, some believe there is nobility in pain, but I do not endorse that perspective.' I caught the scent of the deep vanilla-like aroma of nearby white gardenias – ironically, the flower of joy and happiness.

'You mean Byron's view of the "great object of life being sensation, even if it be in pain"?'

'No, the Catholic elevation of suffering; I am a convert to the religion, but I prefer happiness over hurt – and joy in this world, not the next one.'

He laughed, low and throaty. 'Yet another reason I avoid all religion; I have witnessed too much injustice to believe it is redeemed by a lofty end after death. *This* life is meant to be rich and full, nor do I believe anyone is punished for taking all of the delights that lie at our fingertips.'

'Indeed, no matter what Gaetano did in his life – good or bad – he did not deserve to die alone, perhaps at the hand of some assailant.' My thoughts shifted to his last moments when he took a sudden, final gasp as he collapsed to the floor. So terrible, so tragic. 'At least Elisa will probably never know there was anything suspicious about her husband's death.'

'Nor are we likely to ever find out the truth,' Trelawny mused.

'But you must admit that considering the events of the last few days and what we have learned about the Costa brothers, his demise must be connected somehow with what he was about to reveal to us.'

Trelawny scanned the dense garden with a quick swivel of his head from side to side. 'He was the final link to his two brothers and what happened all those years ago. Sadly, one by one, each of them has perished, perhaps deliberately eliminated, leaving us with nowhere to turn and no one to ask. The truth died with them.' He turned toward me. 'And I feel compelled to add that I have a growing concern someone has always been a step ahead of us on this quest, making certain that whenever we closed in on the facts, we were blocked from going any further. If the three brothers were involved in some kind of plot against Byron that may have involved harming Allegra, they are all gone now. Stefano died in Greece, Father Gianni was murdered in Florence, and now Gaetano, passed away from suspicious causes. There is no one else . . . except whoever wants to prevent us from achieving our goal.'

My chest fell in disappointment tinged with fear as his words sank in. 'The worst part is maybe much of this wretchedness could have been avoided if Father Gianni had been honest with me at the start. He must have known from the moment I asked him for help to find Allegra that she had, indeed, survived. When he wrote to the abbess, it was to silence her. How could he have been so cruel when he knew how much it meant to me to know what happened to my daughter? I shall never, ever excuse him.'

'I admit that it is hard to defend him, Claire, but he may have had his reasons.'

'Nothing warrants such duplicity,' I grated out. As a wave of anger rose up inside of me, I snapped off a red rose bud that grew next to a bench and tossed it into the dirt. 'He was yet another man who had torn apart my dearest wishes, leaving me with the bitter fragments of what might have been. A broken vow that hurt beyond belief. What could justify such a betrayal?'

'I cannot pretend to know his heart, but I do know what it means to do the wrong thing for the right reasons.' He flickered a regretful glance over me. 'It now seems obvious that Father Gianni was connected with this conspiracy he had formed with his brothers, so he may have feared that you would be exposed to some kind of danger once you suspected Allegra had survived. If that were the case, he was probably trying to protect you. Unfortunately, Matteo stabbed him before we could grasp the full story.'

My ire dissipated slightly as I took in Trelawny's speculations. 'Granted, if you are right, Father Gianni was in an impossible situation, but he still had no right to make that choice for me. I would have gladly faced any kind of peril for

Allegra's sake and should have been given the opportunity to decide for myself. He was a priest, not God.'

And I suffered the consequences.

Trelawny sighed deeply. 'Also, just a man who, like any other, had made mistakes and tried his best to navigate a complicated world—'

'You pity him?' I asked in disbelief.

'I sympathize with him.'

'Well, I do not.' Averting my eyes, I took in the darkening sky as night began to fall. Massive gray clouds drifted in from the west and hovered over the city, foreshadowing a dark and moonless evening. 'He should have to answer for his treachery.'

'He died in a horribly violent manner. Is that not enough?'

A thin chill started to settle in, clinging to the edge of his words. In truth, Father Gianni had been my confidante for many years, and I mourned the loss of the person who always advised me when my soul was troubled – a kind and true friend. Until he betrayed me.

'I am not normally tolerant of weakness, but I also do not want you to dismiss all of the light he brought to your life just because he made an error of judgment in this one instance. From everything you told me, he seemed a decent man.'

'Indeed, he was . . . and I needed to be reminded of it.' A tiny spark of wistfulness lit inside of me again, melting away some of the anger. I picked up the rose again and held it in my palm, rubbing its soft, velvety petals. 'When I returned to Florence over a decade ago, it had been so long since I lived there that I no longer knew anyone, and it was Father Gianni who paved the way for me to be introduced into Florentine society. Oh, there were the usual whispers about my illicit past, but he made certain I was invited to local gatherings during feast days and festivals, and, gradually, I became accepted as a respectable English expatriate with many new friends. Not that my own countrywomen were always so kind – there were too many rumors about my relationship with Byron – but, still, they showed civility to me, for Father Gianni's sake. Without his support, my life would have been a great deal more isolated, even with Paula and Georgiana.'

'He would not have cast away such regard so lightly,'

Trelawny mused. 'Only a dire threat against you could have caused him to be so secretive. Matteo killed Father Gianni because of his greed, but there must have been someone else who was drawn out when you asked for the priest's help to find Allegra. The person blocking our quest. He followed us here, perhaps with Matteo's knowledge, and now has been trying to frighten us enough to end our quest with savage acts of vandalism and threats. And he must have known what Gaetano was about to reveal and dispatched him before he could pass it on—'

'Effectively cutting off our last avenue,' I added with a deep sigh, hugging my arms close as a brisk breeze picked up. 'He probably realized that he was in danger by talking with you but did so anyway.'

'Possibly.' Trelawny removed his jacket and placed it around my shoulders.

As I pulled it tightly around me, a woodsy fragrance enveloped my senses like the warm heart of a cypress tree. Earthy and aromatic. Both familiar and reassuring. It contrasted with the sweet scent of the rose that I still held in my hand. 'Whatever else he kept hidden, it died with him and, with it, all hope of unraveling the brothers' conspiracy.'

'Then again, we know enough.' He spoke slowly, reflectively. 'And, if my conjectures are correct, we might need to reconsider your misgivings . . . about Raphael.'

A tiny alarm rang inside of me. 'What do you mean?'

'Just that he has been with us from the beginning, privy to every conversation, every plan. I do not want to believe it, but I cannot discount the possibility he passed that information on to Matteo and, then, maybe took matters into his own hands after Matteo's death.'

'To the point of committing murder?' I shook my head violently. 'No, there must be some other culprit – a criminal who was part of Matteo's network. Baldini himself presented that possibility as well.' Taking a few moments to compose my thoughts, I continued, 'I admit that I doubted Raphael when he hesitated to marry Paula, perhaps even deemed that his poverty might have driven him to swindle us. But that is a far cry from speculating that he might have been involved in or carried out a murder. Surely you are not suggesting that Raphael is a killer.'

He said nothing, but a nightingale suddenly cried out with a shrill, staccato song.

There has to be some other explanation. If we condemn Raphael, we also doom Paula to lose her dream of love.

'Trelawny, we must focus on what we know for certain about the past before we project into the future – the events in Ravenna, the voyage on the *Hercules* . . .' A sudden thought occurred to me. 'You never said what happened after you docked at Cephalonia while Byron planned the Greek invasion. Were there any suspicious incidents?'

'Not really.' He hesitated. 'We worked day and night with few breaks because there was much to be completed before we could sail to Greece. I think Pietro joined Gaetano in the typical activities of young men in a foreign city, but I had no time for revelry. In September of 1823, I traveled ahead to Tripolitza to meet with the Greek revolutionary Odysseas Androutsos, and we spent months preparing for Byron's eventual landing. But Gaetano remained in Cephalonia throughout the fall; I have no idea what occurred there after I left. When Byron eventually landed in Missolonghi after the new year, Gaetano was not with him.'

'And no one mentioned him to you afterwards?'

Trelawny lifted a brow in irony. 'I was a little occupied with the revolution to pay attention even if they did.'

'Of course, but there had to be an event that stood out—'

'Claire – stop,' he cut in as he took my hands, crushing the rose beneath my fingers. 'I am sorry all of this has happened since we came to Ravenna, and that I felt obligated to share my newfound misgivings about Raphael, but can we set all of these troubles aside for just a few moments and simply enjoy being in a garden with such beauty all around us? We used to be able to snatch a bit of bliss even in the darkest of times.'

Like that night we shared together in Pisa.

I will always remember it.

Diverted for a few moments, I could not resist adding with some cynicism, 'Yes, even in the midst of the Greek revolution, you still had time to acquire a young wife.'

He stiffened. 'That is unfair – the union with Tarsitsa was politically expedient, a marriage of convenience. She was the Greek leader, Odysseas's, half-sister, so the match guaranteed his loyalty to us when it was difficult to tell which faction would remain trustworthy; we gave him guns, and he provided us with men. I had little to do with her since she was barely out of girlhood, and we formally divorced when the revolution ended, but you know all of that, Claire. Rebellions are messy . . .'

'And women are often casualties in more ways than can be counted.'

'I . . . cared for her, but it was not love; she knew that before we married.' He tilted his head down. 'Why do you mention it now after all of these years?'

I stared at him and exhaled deeply. 'Because even if we try to push the rest of the world outside these gates, the ghosts of all the people whom we have known rise up between us.'

'You have loved other men, and I have loved other women; but, we have a deep bond between us stronger than time itself.' His breath fanned against my hair like a soft caress. 'After what we have just witnessed, there is no point in holding on to any pretense that my feelings are any less intense than they were in our youth. My heart has always been yours. If you had but given me any hope over the years, I would have been by your side in an instant.'

'And now?'

'I am here with you, until you bid me leave.'

Oh, my dear one, help me finish this endless search for my daughter.

Then, stay with me – now and forever.

But I did not say it.

As if in response, the garden around us seemed to grow dim and silent . . . a fading Eden which had bloomed once but was forever gone. The promise of sweet rapture could not last for very long – not at my age, and I was not willing to risk my heart once more. 'I . . . I do not want to end up like Elisa, with my soul torn apart by grief at losing the person who was my whole world. I already experienced that twice in my life, and I do not think I could face it again.'

'When did you ever shy away from risk?'

'After I saw Elisa's face today.' Edging away from Trelawny,
I drew into myself. 'I never want to feel that way again, nor
do I want to see Paula hurt and devastated by the loss of
Raphael. We must think of them now, my friend – that is all
that matters.' My voice had turned sad and quiet.

He did not respond for a long moment; when he did, his
tone held a note of resignation. 'I respect your wishes, Claire,
and will not mention it again. Once we finish with this adventure, I will sail for England to spend my final days in Sussex
with my daughter, Laetitia. She has been most anxious for my
return, so she can fuss over me, and I miss her dearly. I was
hoping that she might come to Italy to join us, but there seems
little point in that now . . .'

It cannot be any other way.

Could it?

For a mad instant, I imagined Trelawny and his daughter
standing next to me on the Ponte Vecchio in Florence, watching
the sunset in the Tuscan hills to the west, the sky brilliantly
shaded in gold and red and yellow, the air fresh and delicately
fragrant with summer flowers. The murmur of the Arno
flowing gently underneath the bridge. Nothing but joy and
happiness.

Trelawny stood and extended a hand to me, bringing all my
fantasies to an abrupt end. 'It is growing late, and we need to
make our way back to the hotel.'

'But we have still not settled the matter of Raphael,' I
protested, slipping the rose in my pocket. I would keep it as
a memento of Santa Eufemia who had sacrificed so much for
her faith – and my own hard choice to leave my feelings
behind.

'I think it best for now to just remain vigilant as we travel
to Florence, then Livorno,' he said flatly, all emotion under
control once more. Trelawny had become the soldier again,
taking command of the situation with a brusque practicality.

Was I a fool after all?

I swallowed hard as I took his arm. 'Considering the possible
danger that awaits us in Livorno, I believe it will be best if
we leave Paula and Georgiana in Florence, along with Raphael.

And I can ask Lieutenant Baldini to watch Raphael, just as a precaution.'

'She will not like it.'

'She will hate it, but it must be done.'

As we slowly exited the garden, I knew my last chance at love gradually faded away with every step like that song of the nightingale when he disappeared into the sky. Perhaps I should have given in to my feelings for Edward and accepted whatever happiness could be found at this stage in our shared history together. I was tempted, even now. But resurrecting these old desire also raised the specter of the man who always stood between us. Byron. It would stir up too many emotions. Too much hurt. Too much loss.

All that truly remained was the quest that had brought us here and the road that lay ahead.

Silently, we strolled back to the Al Cappello, and I took my leave of Trelawny, knowing I had disappointed him irrevocably. Nothing could repair that wound; it was best to finish packing, return to Florence, and pretend it had never happened. But as I let myself into my room, I could not bring myself to place the last of my belongings in the trunk. Instead, I retrieved the stack of Pietro's letters and flipped through them until I found the last one dated in Cephalonia. There might be something he mentioned about Gaetano that Trelawny had not recalled.

The toymaker now seemed to be the linchpin to ending this journey.

10 December 1823
Metaxata, Cephalonia

My dearest sister,

I long for the day when we can leave this wretched island.

It seems we have been here forever, talking about war when we want to be on the battlefield.

Instead, we talk and plan and scheme; no one knows when we will finally depart.

The constant earthquakes that we experienced in October have started up again, and sometimes the violent shaking goes on for hours, causing the palazzo walls to crack with jagged lines from floor to ceiling. Last night, we had to take refuge in the courtyard below where we remained until dawn. I was too frightened to sleep, but Byron calmly wrapped himself in a tartan cloak and dozed until the sun rose, declaring himself quite rested. Afterwards, though, he said he would endure any future tremors in his own bed. I agreed.

You asked me in your last letter how he is faring, and I cannot answer that question. Some days, he seems quite content, dealing with the various English officials and Greek rebels who come and go, but then he drinks heavily in the evenings, constantly fretting about the state of the revolution and the health of his daughter, Ada, back in England with his estranged wife. The child has a delicate constitution, and he does not want her to experience the same fate as Allegra.

The weight of the world is on his shoulders.

We try to help him but, like all leaders, he must carry this burden alone.

Trelawny has gone on ahead to Tripolitza, and we receive daily updates from him on the state of affairs with the various warring Greek factions, all vying for power. It seems an officer named Mavrocordatos has emerged as the most likely commander – stable and clear-headed. Byron likes him, so it is probable that he will have the support of the London Greek Committee. We hope to join him soon . . . in the meantime, we still have Tita and Byron's physician, Dr Bruno, with us, as well as Gaetano and Vitalis.

All of us live in the same house, as if we were a family.

And I have found solace in my friendship with Gaetano. We swim and laugh and sing together. He is always cheerful, drawing sketches of our life here, even when our situation grows tedious and wearisome. However, Vitalis is another matter. He is the outsider: dour, often foul-tempered, when out of Byron's earshot. Yet he remains on Cephalonia, constantly exploring the old ruins and abandoned villas littered around the island. Gaetano said he is obsessed with finding artifacts that might have

*some value. I believe it since he has shown a keen interest
in ancient art and architecture. Certainly, he has not
stayed because he wants to be involved in Byron's military
campaign.*

*When I asked Gaetano how they came to travel
together, he said they met by chance in a coach en route
to Livorno when Vitalis was looking for a travel
companion on his journey to Greece, and Gaetano wanted
to witness the Greek war first-hand. Luckily, they were
both able to find passage on the* Hercules.

I believed him, but it seemed an odd coincidence.

*Then again, I have to remind myself that with all of
the spies who lurk in every dark corner of Cephalonia,
there are also men of honor and loyalty, and, surely,
Gaetano is one of them. He has now declared his allegiance to the Greek cause and will not desert us when
we finally embark on this bold endeavor.*

Friends and comrades-in-arms.

Three days later . . .

*The most astonishing thing has happened: we are set to
depart for Missolonghi in a few weeks!*

*Apparently, Prince Mavrocordatos sailed there with
the Greek fleet, seizing the role of commander-in-chief,
and he is ready to fight the Turkish troops who have
the town under siege. Our days of glory will begin
soon. We are to join him as soon as Byron can arrange
for passage, and I am almost unbearably excited at
the prospect of finally seeing battle.*

*We will be bringing supplies on behalf of the London
Greek Committee, and I am in charge of making certain
that all of it is loaded on to the ships, especially the
secret war chest of gold that belongs to Byron. I told
only Gaetano about the treasure, but I know he will keep
my confidence.*

Many men would kill for that kind of bounty.

*Even though Byron will deny it, he is almost single-
handedly financing the revolution and inspiring new*

recruits to join the rebels. If you could see him, my dear
sister, you would be so proud. He is decisive and focused,
ready to lay down his life for his beliefs.

Last night, after dinner, he asked playfully whether
it was better to build *a nation than* write *about it, and*
he declared himself one of the long line of poets who
had become soldiers:
Garcilaso de la Vega.
Ewald Christian von Kleist.
Karl Theodor Körner.
Vasili Zhukovsky.
I simply listened as he recited their names, not knowing
any of them. Byron confessed he admired that they all
eventually chose to be men of action over men of words.

Later, when I told Tita about the list of poets, his face
darkened as he said grimly, 'They all died in battle. Byron
does not believe he will return from this war.'

But I dismissed the melancholy thought. I know that
Byron will emerge victorious and return to you as the
liberator of Greece. All of the world will admire his
courage and sacrifice—

I stopped reading, letting the yellowed, wrinkled parchment
flutter to the floor. Then, with a quivering hand, I removed
my spectacles and set them on the tea table. I could no longer
read because my eyes had welled up with tears at the thought
of Byron preparing for a war from which he would never
return. He knew it. I had always wondered whether he had
thrown himself into the fray of revolution with his typical
recklessness or cautious deliberation. From Pietro's account,
it seemed the latter, along with a sense of fatalism about his
own survival.

It both saddened and heartened me.

Byron bore the knowledge of his own possible death with
grim determination, and I applauded that he rose above the
angry, tortured man whom I knew in Geneva. He had been
fighting his entire life – the battlefield of having a deformity
and the war of confronting his own erratic emotions. Mostly,
he suffered defeat on both fronts. Who would have thought

such a lonely, embittered poet could find redemption in an actual war? But it somehow seemed fitting. All of his triumphs and trials came together at Missolonghi, a swampy backwater of a town where, ironically, he raised the banner of freedom for the world.

Bowing my head, I honored his sacrifice for the first time in my life.

Oh, my love, I wish I could have seen you one last time . . . standing on the bow of the ship that took you to your destiny.

Seeing you through Pietro's eyes has healed the last of my hurting soul. No more burning rage and fury – only love.

I freely forgive you for all of the wrongs that you did to me. All that is left is to find Allegra, and I will be at peace.

I would honor your loyalty to liberty, and Trelawny's loyalty to me.

And see this quest through to its end.

Not bothering to remove my dress, I lay on the bed and waited for the dawn.

EIGHT

'I strive to number o'er what days
Remembrance can discover,
Which all that life or earth displays
Would lure me to live over . . .'

Byron, 'All is Vanity, Saith the Preacher,' 9–12

En route to Florence, Italy
July 1873

The next morning, we set out early for the two-day trip to Florence, and it proved to be a hot and dusty route until we entered the Tuscan Apennines. Then the air turned cooler, smelling of pine and moss, as we headed into the mountains. Paula, Georgiana, and I endured the stuffy interior of the carriage while Raphael sat up top with the driver and Trelawny rode alongside on horseback. As I watched my old friend keep up a brisk pace in the saddle, mile after mile, I felt a twinge of guilt. He must be fatigued after making all the travel arrangements and overseeing our departure, but one would never know it from his stoic, straight-backed posture.

A soldier's indomitable will.

Yet he was still somewhat vexed with me.

During the flurry of travel preparations, he had not spoken more than a dozen words to me in a brusque tone, so I had no chance to share what I had read in Pietro's letter. Granted, there seemed little urgency, so my conversation with him could wait until we arrived in San Godenzo for an overnight stop, but I wished that he would relent in his attitude because I did not want our last days together to be contentious.

'Aunt Claire, you seem preoccupied.' Paula's voice softly drifted through my musings. 'You have not said more than a few sentences since we left Ravenna. Did something happen last night when you and Trelawny went out for a *passeggiata*? I know you picked up my mended dresses, but did anything else occur?'

Glancing at my niece's delicate features drawn tight in concern as she held Georgiana close, I smiled in reassurance. 'Nothing remarkable. The toymaker's store was closed, so I could not buy a puzzle for Georgiana. Then, we simply took a stroll and ended up lingering for a short while in a garden near the Via Cavour . . . quite a pretty spot to watch the sunset.'

Ah, that deceit should take such gentle shape . . .

But I could not tell her the whole truth – yet. Not until we knew for certain.

'I see.' She took a quick peep at Georgiana who had dozed off about an hour before, then flashed me a knowing glance. 'It all makes sense now.'

The carriage jolted hard over a bumpy section of the road, masking my reaction. 'What do you mean?'

'Trelawny was unusually silent before we departed, and you have not said more than a handful of words during the entire day. Not to mention the tension between both of you seemed as thick as a morning fog in the Tuscan hills – all of this after a few stolen moments in a romantic garden.' She folded her arms across her chest. 'That could mean only one thing: he must have asked you to marry him . . . and you turned him down.'

I felt a deep flush rise to my face. 'It was not exactly a proposal, rather a declaration of his feelings.'

'You make it seem so . . . prosaic when it was, no doubt, full of passionate intent,' Paula protested.

Eying her, I raised my brows in irony. 'You forget how many seasons I have seen, my dear. The kind of love that I experienced in my youth has somewhat mellowed at this stage of my life.'

'Never.'

I laughed, taking a brief glance at Trelawny's powerfully elegant figure on his horse. 'Certainly, I can still appreciate a handsome face, but I refuse to allow myself to be too beguiled by an attractive man. It almost destroyed me when Byron left, and I do not ever want to feel that kind of desolation again.

Besides, to love with my heart and soul, as I once did, would mean surrendering my hard-won independence. I simply have too much to lose—'

'You are speaking nonsense,' Paula interjected quickly. 'Before Trelawny arrived in Florence, you were bored beyond belief. You said it many times to me. In fact, I was quite concerned after you sprained your ankle that you would never leave your bedchamber again, but then Mr Rossetti appeared with the news about Allegra and you became revived. Almost youthful. Truly, there are many ways of dying, and I think the worst is believing that life can give you nothing beyond a dull, spiritless routine. It kills you slowly. I know what it is like to have my heart broken, but I refuse to lock up my emotions in a prison of fear and cynicism – nor should you.'

'Oh, my dear, you are so wise. In spite of all the danger and hardships over the last couple of weeks, I would not have missed this adventure for all the world. The prospect of finding my darling Allegra *has* renewed my spirits beyond all imagining – truly, I am so grateful to all of you.' Sighing, I turned away from the window. 'But when it ends, Trelawny will return to England and I will remain in Florence. We are not meant to be together, other than as friends.'

Star-crossed, would-be lovers.

But Trelawny and I still cared deeply for each other; our interlude in the garden last night proved it to me.

And it stirred my recollections again of our brief encounter all those years ago.

I would never forget the feel of his body next to mine that night in Pisa after Shelley died and we came together as two lost souls. I remembered as he drew my long, dark hair across his chest, murmuring soulful words of desire. I remembered the fragrance of jasmine that drifted through the room on that hot summer night. I remembered the sound of his breathing as a cloudy dawn arrived and I stole off before he awakened.

I remembered it all as if it had just been a mere breath away.

'All I can say is that Trelawny's devotion to you is touching, and I would not dismiss it so lightly, any more than I would throw away the love I share with Raphael,' she said firmly. 'Such love is the guiding light to joy and happiness.'

I fervently hope so – for your sake, my dear niece.

Quickly, I lowered my eyes, knowing that Paula's sharp perceptions would see my reaction – and maybe even sense my doubts again. I prayed for her sake that he was not playing her false.

'You have become pensive again, Aunt, which must mean that I have struck a chord inside of you about Trelawny.' Paula nuzzled Georgiana and softly lay her cheek against her daughter's head, careful not to wake her. 'In time, I believe that you will come to regret not following your heart.'

'The time for that kind of life is long past.'

'Never.'

We said nothing more on the subject as our carriage rolled on with a steady rhythm, climbing higher in the mountains with a changing landscape of beech and oak trees, which formed a canopy over deep ravines, dotted with random purple and pink foliage. Waterfalls. Spidery plants. Massive rock outcroppings. A wild beauty.

Stirring and wonderous.

As the road took on a steep and narrow angle, I saw Trelawny fall back to ride behind the carriage. But I could still hear his horse panting in the thin mountain air. It would not be long until we arrived in San Godenzo. And then on to Florence in the morning. In the meantime, I decided to let Paula interpret my silence as she chose and wait to share any misgivings until I could speak with Lieutenant Baldini . . .

Georgiana finally stirred slightly in her mama's arms. As her eyes fluttered open, she gazed up at Paula and asked, *'Siamo arrivati?'*

She smiled at her. 'Yes, we are almost there.'

And one day closer to the reckoning in Livorno.

By late afternoon, we arrived in San Godenzo, nestled between the dense woods and mountains. The town, perched on the top of a hill, was comprised of a smattering of Tuscan-style buildings spaced at close angles and all painted white with clay-colored roofs. In the central piazza, a belltower rose above an old monastery, its clock barely visible above the surrounding rooflines. Such a quiet charm after the frenetic days in Ravenna.

Turning west, we headed down a cypress-lined lane and then halted in front of a rustic inn of weathered stone – plain and neatly landscaped with a profusion of bright red poppies. A wooden sign stood out front: *Casa dei Fiori Rossi.* House of the Red Flowers.

A middle-aged woman with strong features and a kind smile appeared at the front door. She wore a simple white cotton dress, her thick, curling hair loose around her shoulders like a silvery cobweb. As she moved forward, she greeted us in Italian: 'I am Francesca Abbadelli – the owner.'

'*Buongiorno, Signora,*' Trelawny said, dismounting and tying the reins to a nearby post. Then he helped Paula and me out of the carriage, lifting a still-sleepy Georgiana into his arms. Raphael joined us and we all trooped inside. Once in the foyer, I took in a deep breath as I arched my back to stretch the tired muscles and rubbed the back of my neck. It had been a long journey.

'Would you like to see your room straightaway?' Signora Abbadelli inquired, looking at me.

'Yes, indeed,' I murmured gratefully, knowing I must look worn and tired. But as I took in the rough, pebbly walls and comfortable, cushioned furniture of the inn, I felt my fatigue fade somewhat at the tranquil surroundings. Perhaps after a short rest, I might be able to enjoy a dinner *con la famiglia.*

'I will settle in Paula with the little one, then Raphael and I can attend to the luggage,' Trelawny proposed.

Georgiana took that moment to become fully awake, and she tugged playfully on his beard for attention. Trelawny laughed and lifted her high above his head while she squirmed in delight. Then he twirled her around before setting her on to the stone floor.

Paula took her hand and glanced at me, as if to say, *You see what you are giving up?*

Deliberately turning my back to my niece, I asked our hostess to lead me to my room, which she did directly: down a narrow, bare hallway that ended with a wooden door, slightly agape. Slowly, I pushed it open, expecting a spartan room, but I was pleasantly surprised to take in a warm and inviting space with an iron bed, oak washstand, and massive stone fireplace – already lit with glowing flames.

'Dinner is at half past eight.' Francesca handed me the key and withdrew, closing the door soundlessly behind her. I took a few turns around the room, then slid into a wingback chair, allowing the hustle and bustle of the trip to fall away gradually as I stared at the burning logs. They crackled with whispering hisses and sudden pops: nature's energy, held within the live trees for centuries, which threw off an unusual odor that smelled like tart cherries at harvest-time. I closed my eyes for just a few seconds of sweet repose . . .

I jolted awake at a loud thudding sound. Taking a quick scan around me, I realized one of the large logs had broken apart in the fireplace and fallen to the side of the grate. Reaching for the iron tongs, I managed to clasp the burning chunk and set it back atop the stack of wood. It flared instantly into a pale flame. Satisfied, I replaced the tool and began to freshen up at the washstand's china basin when I caught sight of my trunk positioned at the foot of the bed, travel bag sitting next to it.

Trelawny.

He must have had it delivered while I slept. Such thoughtful acts were making it more and more difficult for me to imagine his departure, but leave he must.

I tidied my hair and selected my best evening dress to wear, realizing that it would be the last time our little band of travelers dined together before Trelawny and I continued on to Livorno – alone. A special occasion, even if Paula did not know it and, as such, it should be savored since I did not know when we would all be joined again.

Sitting on the bed, I smoothed down the skirt of my cream-colored silk frock lying next to me, noting happily it had not grown too wrinkled in the trunk. It traveled well over long distances, even if I did not. At one time, I could journey all day and then dance all night, but no longer. After hours in a carriage, I now longed only for a short dinner and a soft bed to save my energy for what lay ahead.

Taking a quick glance at the small clock on the fireplace mantle, I realized that I still had half an hour before dinnertime. I grasped my travel bag and rummaged through its contents for Pietro's letter which I had hastily tucked away earlier in the day, still unfinished. Unfolding it, I held the parchment up to the window light . . .

I intend to fight alongside Byron, to the death.

We decided to divide our force between two ships: Byron will take a fast-sailing mistico, so he can anchor in the Missolonghi lagoon, and I will be further offshore on the larger bombard with the servants and supplies. The war chest will be divided between us, so if the Turks capture one of us, the other will have enough gold and other valuables to keep the revolution going.

Gaetano will be with me, but Vitalis is supposed to accompany Byron.

I do not like it, but there was nothing I could do until yesterday when I saw the Greek skulking around both ships when the bulky chests were being loaded.

No doubt, he suspected that we are carrying treasures with us and was trying to confirm the value of our cargo. I shared my observations with Byron, and he finally agreed it was time to part ways with our fellow traveler. Vitalis did not take it well. I overheard him shouting at Tita who simply picked him up and physically threw him out of the door into the courtyard.

I am happy that is the last we will see of Vitalis.

Gaetano did not say much about it, but I could tell that he, too, was relieved.

We depart in three weeks, so pray for me, my dear sister. Pray that the sea voyage goes well. Pray that I acquit myself as a man of courage. Pray that we win the day once we enter the field of battle.

Pray that we survive.

I love you dearly.

Your brother,

Pietro

Still standing at the window, I took a few moments to take stock of the letter's content. My emotions swelled high in admiration for Pietro, for he was everything that I had heard Byron once say about him: 'amiable, brave, and excellent . . . with a thirst for knowledge.' And I was truly sorry that I had never met him. But my curiosity was also stirred by the suggestion that both Vitalis and Gaetano knew about the hoard of riches aboard each ship, which might explain why they initially secured passage with Byron's voyage to Cephalonia: to discover the treasure's location and take it for themselves.

A more likely motivation than to harm Byron.

Yet, from everything that Pietro related about him, Gaetano did not strike me as a thief. And surely Elisa would have known if her husband had forfeited all sense of duty and honor for ill-gotten wealth? They had spent a lifetime together.

Most puzzling, though, was how the other two brothers, Stefano and Father Gianni, fit into this plot.

Even now, I found it difficult to believe that my beloved priest had been involved at all.

Rubbing my temples with a sudden sense of weary frustration, I tossed the letter aside and rang for a servant to help me change my dress. I would give Trelawny the letter and see if he could decipher something I had missed, because it seemed the more I learned, the less I actually knew, with none of the information connected to Allegra in any way whatsoever.

Maddening.

Not long afterwards, I made my way to the dining room and encountered Trelawny just outside its brick archway; he wore an evening suit, the waistcoat and trousers neatly pressed. Quite stylish.

I handed him the letter, quickly relating what I had just read while keeping a wary eye for Paula's appearance.

Trelawny drew me aside. 'I have to say I am surprised by Pietro's speculations, especially about Vitalis; as I mentioned, he seemed almost a comical figure, as I recall. But I spent little time in his company, so Pietro may have seen a side of him that I did not. And it is quite true that most Cephalonians knew Byron personally financed much of the war since he signed a very public loan in Argostoli to the Greeks. Anyone had ample opportunity to learn about the precious cargo.'

'It would seem so,' I readily agreed. 'When you and Byron met up again in Greece, was the war chest intact?'

'Yes, and Byron counted every coin.' Leaning against the wall, he slipped the letter into his jacket pocket. 'Let me think on it.'

'Could you send a note to Lieutenant Baldini that I want to meet with him tomorrow after we arrive in Florence? Around noon in the Boboli Gardens near the obelisk – he will know where, of course.'

The place where Byron and I had buried the lock of Allegra's hair, sacred until Matteo tried to kill us there. It now held bittersweet memories, but I had to see it one last time.

'I shall. We can depart for Livorno directly afterwards,' he proposed. 'How do you want to tell Paula that we are leaving her and Georgiana behind?'

I chewed on my lip, weighing my options, but none of them seemed appealing. 'I . . . am not sure yet, but they must remain in Florence, along with the Cades sketch which we can leave in my bank's vault. Unlike the trip to Ravenna when we believed ourselves to be safe, we know the journey to Livorno could be fraught with danger.'

'Indeed, we shall have to be very careful . . .'

At that moment, Paula strolled up with Raphael alone, explaining that she had already given Georgiana her dinner and put her to bed. The young couple had donned their best attire, as well, and looked quite refreshed, their faces relaxed and animated as they chatted about the bracing mountain air. 'Aunt, do you not savor this cool breeze after the heat and dust of the road?' she inquired, tucking a tiny scarlet poppy in her upswept curls. 'It is so pleasant.'

'It is a rustic idyll.' A bit overstated, but just seeing Paula look so blissful gladdened my heart considerably. 'Shall we go in?'

As they nodded and moved past us, I began to follow in their wake when I heard a hushed whisper in my ear, 'If I have not said so in a while, you look lovely, Claire . . . Beauty's Daughter – forever.'

My lips curved upwards in delight, then I took his arm. 'Thank you, my friend. I thought you might still be upset with me.'

'Oh, make no mistake, I am . . . disappointed, but I do not want to waste a beautiful evening in the Italian mountains.' He smiled down at me – albeit sadly. 'We may never be here again and should savor it before we all go our separate ways.'

And savor it we did.

It proved to be a magical evening, almost as if the Casa dei Fiori Rossi had slipped delicately out of time, allowing us to step out of our careworn journey and cherish every minute without a concern about the next stage. For once, I did not want to think about tomorrow; it would come soon enough.

I wanted tonight for all of us.

Our buoyant mood lasted while Francesca served a *primo* of creamy pecorino cheese and a *secondo* of spicy sausages with Tuscan grapes, accompanied by a local Chianti that tasted like wild berries. Lastly, she set out *buccellato* for dessert – a soft pastry with raisins and nuts. All simple dishes with their sweet and savory tastes blending in each course. I could not ask for more. While we enjoyed our meal, our hostess entertained us with tales of the many travelers who had stopped at her inn, most of which had some amusing aspect.

'Do you operate this inn alone, Signora?' I inquired as I finished my glass of wine. 'It seems a daunting task for a single woman.'

'Especially in such a remote place,' Paula added.

'*Sì*. I manage everything myself since my husband died six years ago, though my son comes once a week to deliver food and sundries.' She poured us each a cup of coffee – a rich, dark liquid. 'It does not feel isolated with a household of two servants to supervise, fields to plant, and cows to milk. I am occupied every day. And the vast mountains are my friends; they nourish me, *corpo e anima* – body and soul.'

It sounded like a lonely existence.

Much as I enjoyed being in nature, I loved the energy of Florence. Whenever I was away from it too long, I felt my own vitality fade a bit; I needed to be in the flow of human activity – hearing the bells of the *Cattedrale di Santa Maria del Fiore* and smelling the delicious Tuscan foods that emanated from the cafés. *La bella vita.* Too much silence felt oppressive to me, especially now that I had entered my own autumnal years. My friends and family kept me rooted in the world of the living with sweet bonds of tenderness and affection.

Francesca handed a cup to my niece. 'I also have the memories of my husband; they never fade, even though he is no longer with me.'

Ah, yes, living with a shadow companion.
Walking with ghosts from the past.
Dreaming of days long gone.

It could be uncomfortable at times to have such reminders of loss and grief, but impossible to bid farewell to them.

Paula must have been thinking along similar lines about Georgiana's absent father, because she flicked a brief, nervous glance at Raphael who caressed her cheek in response. She turned her face toward his palm and nuzzled it. Knowing he meant to reassure her, I gritted my teeth to stop myself from uttering a cautionary comment. That would accomplish nothing, except push Paula further away from me.

Instead, I sipped my coffee and let the rest of the evening unfold in pleasant gaiety.

When I returned to my room, the jubilant mood still lingered as I hummed and repacked my trunk for an early morning departure. Halfway through my task, I spied a handful of red poppies attached to a note on my pillow with only a few scrawled lines:

> *Viaggiare con Dio.*
> *Francesca*

Travel with God.
    My dearest wish, as well.

By morning, we set out under gloomy skies. As the carriage creaked out of the mountains, thin streaks of sunlight peeped through the clouds like lancets pointing the way to our destination in Florence: the Palazzo Cruiciato. The place that had become more of a home than anywhere I had ever lived. It pained me that I could stay only a few hours, but it was best not to wait. It would only make leaving Paula and Georgiana that much harder for me.

When we pulled up outside my apartment at the palazzo on the Via Romana, I almost clapped with relief at the familiar sight of its decaying façade of stone blocks and high-vaulted windows. *La mia casa.*

'We are home, Georgiana. *La nostra casa,*' Paula exclaimed as she flung open the carriage door. Alighting on her own with an eager step, she then lifted her daughter out. 'It seems as if we have been gone for *ages.*'

'Much too long.' I managed to exit the vehicle myself and shook out my skirt; a soft drizzle had begun to fall. 'I will have Trelawny handle the luggage, and, perhaps after we air out the apartment, you and Raphael can visit the market with Georgiana while I take a short walk to stretch my aging joints.'

'But, first, I must speak with Matteo's aunt about my new duties,' Raphael proposed. 'Then, I shall be happy to accompany Paula.'

'Perfect – it should not take too long to straighten out our rooms.'

We ushered Georgiana inside, and as we made our way up the stairs to the third floor, I could hear Trelawny giving orders to have Paula's trunk taken down. Mine would remain. But she had already climbed all the flights and did not catch his instructions, which would make it simpler for me to complete my business and be on my way again without her being any the wiser.

In scarcely an hour, Paula and I had opened windows, swept the floors, and dusted the furniture. The musty, stagnant odor had already been replaced by the clean, pure smell of summer rain and freshly polished wood. Taking stock of our work, I scanned the high-ceilinged parlor with satisfaction. Everything stood in order, from my books positioned in neat rows on the bookshelves to the carefully stacked mail on my writing desk. I could leave Paula in charge now.

It would be *her* place.

After a short knock at the front door, Trelawny entered with my small travel case in hand; he set it on one of the wingback chairs near the fireplace. 'I heard from Lieutenant Baldini, and

he would like to have a few words with you at the Boboli
Gardens, Claire, if you are up to it. I can escort you there.'

'That would be lovely since I intended to take a stroll there
anyway.' I retrieved the cup-and-ball toy out of my bag and
set it out for Georgiana, but she was too distracted, tugging
on Paula's sleeve and complaining that she was hungry. 'Why
not take her for lunch with Raphael, and you can stop at the
market on the way back?'

'That will take hours.' Her eyes narrowed slightly. 'Is there
anything wrong? Have you changed your mind about going
to Livorno?'

'No, I still intend to travel there, but I was thinking about
you and Georgiana right now.'

'I appreciate that, but you seem a bit distracted.' She glanced
back and forth between Trelawny and me. 'Are you sure there
is nothing amiss?'

'Just tired.'

Georgiana stomped her foot. '*Mama, ho fame.*'

'Yes, yes, I know you are famished.' Paula took her hand.
'Come along. We will collect Raphael on the way to the *trat-
toria* down the street.'

As Georgiana dragged her to the entrance, I caught Paula's
arm. 'Thank you, my dear, for accompanying me on my flight
of fancy to Ravenna, putting up with my stubborn ways, and
extending to me a thousand other niceties; you are so like
your father, Charles. I know I can be trying, yet you have been
unfailingly kind, and I appreciate it more than I can say. Truly.'

She responded with a brief embrace. 'It is I who am grateful
for your generosity and love. Papa would have been so happy
to know we found such solace in each other. When I return
from the market, we will start planning for the next stage of
our journey—'

'Mama!'

Paula rolled her eyes, then quickly exited with Georgiana
– and, just like that, they were both gone.

Would I ever see them again?

Trelawny closed the door behind them with a sense of
finality and then turned toward me with a somber expression.
'Beautifully done, Claire. I am in awe of your courage when

it would have been so much easier to tell Paula what you intend to do.'

'She would never accept it.' But I had charted my course and would not turn back now. 'It should not take me more than an hour to meet with Baldini, and he can bring me back. I will relate everything that occurred in Ravenna and give him the stickpin. Perhaps he will have some news about the *cinquedea* and information about Raphael.'

'While you are with the lieutenant, I will obtain fresh horses for the carriage, leave the Cades drawing at your bank and be ready to depart as soon as you are finished.' He started for the door, then paused. 'Are you sure that you do not need more time to rest before you see Baldini?'

I shook my head as I handed him the sketch. 'I am ready – now.'

Without further discussion, we made our way out of the palazzo and along the crowded Via Romana toward the nearby Pitti Palace on the south side of the Arno River. As we approached the familiar sight, I was struck, as always, by the rusticated stonework which created a severe, doleful appearance. The original builder, Luca Pitti, had wanted to create a building very different from the graceful Florentine architecture of the Renaissance, but he quickly tired of it and sold it to the powerful Medici family. Oddly, they left the rough façade intact.

But they added the Boboli Gardens behind it – the exquisite complex of lovely meadows, fountains, and flowering trees. A breathtaking blend of art and nature. I particularly liked the Roman statues placed along *Il Viottolone* – Cypress Lane . . . and, of course, the obelisk.

After Trelawny left me at the side entrance to the garden, I walked slowly through the archway, into the large courtyard which opened on to the wide, circular expanse of a flat, grassy area; at the center stood the obelisk: the fifteen-foot, needle-shaped structure brought in 1790 from the Medicis' villa in Rome. A symbol of power, reaching into the sky with unobstructed strength.

It stood guard over the garden complex.

And it meant something much more personal to me . . .

In 1822, six months after Allegra had supposedly died, Byron met me here and confessed his guilt and regret over leaving her in the convent. He had aged in the intervening six years since I had seen him last – pale and thin, his hair threaded with gray.

He was to leave for Greece but wanted to see me before he departed on the *Hercules*, so we could bury a tiny box that contained one of Allegra's precious curls at the base of the obelisk.

We spoke little, except for his entreaty: *Promise me, Claire, that you will never look at the box again – or grieve for our daughter endlessly . . . You have many years ahead of you, I think, and you must not lose that love of life that so entranced me.*

Sadly, he omitted to add that attached to the lock of hair was a secret note in which he revealed that Allegra had survived the typhus, adding: *You will never see these words, or know that I truly loved you.*

But how could he have cared about me and carried out such a deception?

It now seemed he had reasons that were beyond what I could have imagined at the time, and which I still did not fully understand.

When I drew near the obelisk, I spied Baldini already standing there, hands shoved in his police uniform pockets as he stared fixedly at its pointed tip, shooting upward like a sword trying to split apart the dark skies.

'It seems we have gathered in this spot before,' I commented, remembering the last time, when Matteo had tried to kill me. 'It all began here, did it not?'

'*Sì.*' He swung his pensive gaze in my direction. 'The hard Egyptian stone has born witness to many human tragedies, but it remains eternal.'

'Like life itself?'

'*E sempre stato cosi* – it was always like this.'

A large drop of rain splashed against my head, and I caught sight of massive black clouds that had formed overhead. Quickly, I reached into my bag and retrieved the stickpin, still swathed in my delicately embroidered handkerchief. 'I believe

Trelawny sent you a letter from Ravenna telling you how he and I found this jewel buried in the body of a dead fox outside Teresa Guiccioli's villa.'

'*Sì*.' Taking it, Baldini carefully unwound the cotton square and turned mute as he looked at the stickpin. 'I can only say I am sorry that you have been the victim of such cruel intimidation, but it seems to support what I have found in my inquiry about the *cinquedea*. Do you recall when Matteo first brought me to your apartment during my investigation of Father Gianni's murder?'

'Yes, you said that he might have been killed by one of his parishioners . . . perhaps one who was angry about not being able to take back a priceless item he had donated to the basilica,' I said, trying to summon the rest of the details. 'A member of an old Florentine family who had fallen on hard times.'

'Exactly.' He turned the stickpin over in his hand, tracing the ruby jewels with his index finger. 'The engraving on the weapon matched an old coat of arms connected to this same family.'

'But Matteo confessed to stabbing Father Gianni—'

'Which is why we released the man at the time,' he cut in swiftly. 'But he has recently traveled to Ravenna, returning only this morning, which coincided with your trip. I have ordered him to be brought in for questioning again since he may have been Matteo's accomplice.'

Taken aback, I blinked several times. 'Who is it?'

'I cannot say – yet.'

'But at least you must tell me if . . . he is connected in any way to Raphael,' I pressed. 'I must know for Paula's sake, if nothing else.'

'I do not think so.'

I exhaled in relief. At least Raphael appeared to be the honest and forthright young man I took him for when I first met him. I gave a short, silent prayer of thankfulness. I could now leave Paula here with a clear conscience, and let Baldini finish his inquiry.

He wiped the mist from his forehead. 'Signora, you must go indoors; it is not healthy to be in this damp drizzle.' He

re-wrapped the stickpin and slipped it into the pocket of his
jacket. Then he took my elbow and began to steer me quickly
toward the Boboli Gardens' entrance. 'Perhaps we can continue
our conversation this evening, if you are not too fatigued.'

'There is nothing that I would like more, but I am departing
forthwith,' I said, tightening my shawl around my shoulders.
'Paula and Georgiana will remain here, but Trelawny and I
have one last piece of business to finish out of town, so we
must leave within the hour.'

'So soon?' He looked taken aback.

'It is an urgent matter.' I paused under the cover of the
archway and shook out my shawl before donning it again.
'And I trust in your interrogation skills now that you have a
suspect.' Just saying the last word caused me to feel a light-
ness inside which I had not experienced in weeks.

'*Grazie*.' He bowed his head at the compliment. 'At least
let me return you to the Palazzo Cruciato before the rain grows
any heavier.'

'That would be most welcome.' We hurried toward the Via
Romana and joined the rest of the thinning crowd rushing
along the sidewalk for shelter. Baldini kept a tight grip on my
arm as we navigated the slippery stones, and we covered the
short distance before the weather worsened.

'May I ask where you are traveling?' he inquired as we
stood on the front steps.

'I would prefer not to tell you.' I stretched my hand to him.
'That way, you could not be held accountable for anything that
might happen. You have a long career ahead of you, my friend,
and I do not want to put your reputation in jeopardy.'

'As you wish.' He clasped my fingers. '*Ci vediamo presto*.'

'Indeed, I shall see you soon.' I waved goodbye and watched
him disappear into the rain before I went inside to my
apartment.

An hour later, I was ready to depart for Livorno, with only
one task left to complete in the short time left.

I sat at my writing desk and picked up my fountain pen,
dipping it into the silver inkwell that Shelley had given me.
It had been one of my most beloved gifts from him, and I had
kept it all these years; every time I wrote a letter and used it,

I thought of our dear Shelley – his untidy hair, wild eyes, and passionate devotion to poetry. A genius in every sense. And my friend who never deserted me until the day he died.

But sometimes those whom we love leave us – intentionally or not.

Like now.

> *My dear Paula,*
>
> *By the time you see this letter, Trelawny and I will have already left for Livorno. Forgive me for not taking you and Georgiana with us, but I do not wish you to take any more risks on my behalf. I did not tell you that there was a violent incident at Teresa's villa the day we visited her, or that the Ravenna toymaker died under suspicious circumstances, so I have decided that it is best you remain in Florence. You have sacrificed enough.*
>
> *Once we arrive in Livorno, I believe that we will finally learn what happened to Allegra and, if we do, I shall be overjoyed – no matter what the outcome. All I have ever wanted is to know the truth, and that will be enough to assuage my guilt and regret over giving up my daughter all those years ago. As a mother, you know that losing a child is the worst trial a woman can endure.*
>
> *When we return to Florence, we can all celebrate together but, should any misfortune befall us, I want you to have the Cades drawing, which I have left in my bank's vault, and all of my correspondence – as well as this silver inkwell. Mr Rosetti will be arriving shortly to assist with selling the artwork, which should provide enough money for you and Georgiana to have a comfortable life with Raphael.*
>
> *Never doubt that I love you as if you were my own dear daughter. These last years have been some of the happiest in my life because of you and Georgiana.*
>
> *T'amo,*
> *Your loving Aunt Claire*

It was done.

I folded the note and set it atop my Byron/Shelley letters along with the handwritten copy of the poem Byron had written to me during the summer of 1816: 'There Be None of Beauty's Daughters.'

I rigidly held the tears in check.

Then I placed my palms on the desk and pushed myself firmly into an upright position.

Without a backward look, I let myself out of the apartment and into the street below, where Trelawny stood waiting by the open carriage door.

'We should be in Livorno by nightfall,' he vowed, assisting me up the stairs.

'I am ready.'

Once we were settled inside, the driver shouted at the horses, causing the carriage to lurch forward slowly. As I peered out of the window, I caught sight of Paula and Raphael with Georgiana, hurrying down the street behind us, each of them holding a strap of the straw market bag and laughing as a piece of fruit tipped out and rolled into the gutter. Fortunately, they did not see us before we turned the corner.

They would be safe.

Satisfied, I sat back and faced the road ahead.

Convent of San Giovanni, Bagnacavallo, Italy
18 April 1822

Allegra's story . . .

I coughed all through the night.

My lungs burned and my bones ached.

Sister Anna came into my room to check on me several times and, after the last visit, she carried me to the sick room to be attended by a doctor. He listened to my chest and frowned, saying something to Sister Anna that I could not hear.

I wanted Papa.

I wanted *Mammina.*

I wanted Tita.

Why did no one arrive to nurse me, except the nuns?

Moaning as a wave of pain washed over me, I felt so hot that I could hardly breathe, but the doctor insisted that I stay under a heavy blanket. I kept kicking it off, but Sister Anna would always cover me with it again. I begged her to take it away, but she refused.

I rolled my head to the side to see my friend, Antonia. She was also sick and lay motionless in the bed next to mine; her eyes half-closed, she had not made a sound in hours.

'*Allegrina?*' she whispered. 'Are you awake?'

'*Sì.*'

'Can you see the beautiful angel with white wings standing there? I think she means to take me to heaven soon.' She pointed at the foot of her bed.

No one was there.

Antonia dropped her arm and closed her eyes; she turned as pale as stone.

'No, you must remain awake, Antonia,' I exclaimed.

'I . . . I will try,' she said weakly.

Sister Anna approached again with a wooden bowl. 'You must drink some of this broth; it will keep you strong.' She held a spoonful near my mouth and slowly tipped it down my throat. I almost retched.

She set it aside and placed a cool cloth on my forehead.

Then I floated off into a dreamy world where I was running along the beach, watching a seabird skim along the water's surface, and a pretty lady chased me, laughing every time I evaded her clutches. My English *mammina*. But when I reached out to hug her, she transformed into the blinded Jesus figure from the nativity scene. I screamed and awakened to the sight of Sister Anna bent over me while she murmured calming words.

As I tried to focus on her, I noticed the bed was empty. '*Dov'è Antonia?*'

'Her parents came and took her home.' Sister Anna brushed back my damp hair. 'Do not fear because your papa will fetch you, too.'

I cried aloud. 'No one will come for me.'

Clutching my cornetto pendant, I turned away from her and drifted in and out of sleep again, not sure what was real or not. I thought I saw Tita hovering nearby and looking anxious. As if from a long distance, I heard his voice say, 'I hope I am not too late to save her.'

Was I going to die?

NINE

'We repent – we abjure – we will break from our chain,
We will part – we will fly to – unite it again.'

Byron, 'I Speak Not – I Trace Not – I Breathe Not,' 7–8

Livorno, Italy
July 1873

Trelawny was as good as his word, and we arrived in the *Venezia Nuova* of Livorno by nightfall, crossing the Marble Bridge to the Via Borra as the moon rose over the district of rich and imposing palazzos. When I stayed in the city with Mary and Shelley in 1819, we resided three kilometers south of this intricate web of wide canals and twisted avenues; it was not a happy time because Mary had just lost her son, William, to a fever and was in deep mourning. Her desolation had been relieved somewhat by the arrival of my ever-cheerful brother, Charles, but it was not until Mary found she was expecting a child again that the gloom lifted. By that time, we had already left for Florence.

Perhaps this visit would also prove to have a similar positive outcome.

Once the carriage dropped us off, Trelawny and I checked into the Palazzo Marciano, a large, elegant hotel which faced the busy port. By that time, I was so exhausted that I did not pause to take in my surroundings but simply bid him *buonanotte*. The young manager, Sergio, had been expecting us and immediately took me to my third-floor room which turned out to be spacious, with a high ceiling and beautifully appointed furniture.

After he left, I completed a brief toilette and lay on the fluffy pillow and closed my eyes, falling asleep almost instantly.

When I awakened the next day, I started, realizing that it was already mid-morning. I had slept almost ten hours. Flinging back the coverlet, I rang the bell for a servant to bring me a bowl of water. While I waited, I spied a note that had been slipped under my door. Eagerly, I unfolded it and read Trelawny's scrawl: he awaited me in the breakfast room – and had news.

Praise be – I had awaited this day for so long.

I quickly freshened up, dressed in a red-and-white striped taffeta dress and arranged my hair into an upswept style with a matching rose-colored silk ribbon. No sad colors. Only light and joy. Lastly, I clasped the locket around my throat before I made my way downstairs to a small breakfast alcove with frescoed walls and linen-covered tables. Trelawny sat alone, drinking a cup of tea near a large picture window. He stood as I approached and held out the chair for me before he seated himself again.

'What did you find out?' I asked breathlessly as I arranged my skirt in neat folds.

'Do you not want to order first?' he teased.

'Edward.' I fastened my glance on him with deliberated intent. 'I want to know . . . now.'

He leaned forward with a smile. 'Early this morning, I met my old friend who works for the local bank, and he told me where the Gianelli palazzo is located; it is only a short walk from here. He had already contacted Antonia's unmarried daughter who lives there, Bianca, and she has agreed to see us today. Unfortunately, my friend knew nothing about Byron arranging for monetary payments to a priest but said he would inquire with other banks in the city.'

My spirits soared. 'I can scarcely believe it. When do we see her?'

'Around eleven o'clock.'

I gave a little cry of relief, mixed with excitement.

'Claire, I know how much this means to you, but we must be realistic,' he reminded me after he asked the waiter to bring another cup of oolong tea. 'We do not know how the Gianelli family is involved in events related to Allegra. If they have buried any secrets under the weight of so many decades, it is likely they will not reveal too much.'

'I understand.'

The waiter returned with my tea and a plate of Italian pastries. But I was too excited to drink or eat. My mind was already racing with various possibilities, including that of learning that my precious daughter was alive and perhaps living with the Gianelli family. Just the thought made me grow almost faint with anticipation. *My own dear Allegra.*

Mid-fanaticizing, I felt a light touch on my shoulder and I tilted up my head. 'Mr Rossetti! How wonderful to see you again,' I exclaimed in delight. 'Are you staying at the hotel?'

'Indeed, yes.' He embraced me warmly and shook hands with Trelawny. 'I was *en route* to Florence and decided to make a brief detour to see the sculptures in the Church of Saint Ferdinand. On my way, I heard there was an English couple staying at the hotel, so I came to pay my respects. How fortunate it turned out to be such familiar friends.' His pleasant face eased into a smile. 'But do not worry that I will tarry in Livorno. I have already contacted two Florentine art dealers who are interested in the Cades work and will show it to them later this week. If their interest is any indication, it will bring in a considerable sum.'

'I am most grateful,' I said, gesturing for him to join us. 'Is your mother feeling better?'

'She has greatly improved – thank you,' he responded. 'But may I ask why you are in Livorno? I thought we were going to link up in Florence.'

'We had some unfinished business that brought us here, though it may turn out to be a short stay.' I signaled for the waiter to bring another teacup and then launched into a narrative of the recent exploits that had brought us here.

His face took on an expression of astonishment. 'What an incredible story, Miss Clairmont.'

'It all began when you came to Florence to buy my Byron/ Shelley letters, so it seems fitting that you are present for the final outcome of that eventful day.' I gazed out at the wide canal that led to the Ligurian Sea. 'I fervently pray that we have the outcome I have longed for these many years.'

Mr Rossetti placed his hands in a prayer-like posture. 'I wish for that as well.'

'Your sentiments do you credit, sir,' Trelawny added.

We drank our tea and made idle chatter, but my mind was fixed on what awaited us. Would it be the greatest delight or yet another bitter disappointment? I dared not delve too deeply into the former, while I feared the latter. Please, let me at least know that Allegra had lived and tasted the sweetness of a young woman's life and beyond . . .

Trelawny cleared his throat, bringing me back to the present. 'It is time for us to go, but would you care to walk with us, Rossetti? We are heading a short distance along the Via Borra.'

'I would be delighted.' He rose and then assisted me out of my chair. 'It is on my way since Saint Ferdinand's is but a little further south, near the Piazza del Luogo.'

Trelawny settled the bill and then, after a quick scan of the outside surroundings, escorted us on to the main avenue, still partially shaded from the midday sun. As we strolled along the street, I nodded at several passers-by who had also decided to enjoy the beauties of Venezia Nuova, from the imposing palazzos to the stylish boats docked on the canal. A graceful port compared with the brooding decay of Venice, but perhaps it held its own similar secrets.

When we approached a cream-colored, three-storied building with green shutters and massive oak doors, Trelawny halted. As if on cue, the door opened, and a formally outfitted *maggiordomo* appeared who asked, 'Signora Clairmont?'

'*Sì.*' My breath caught in my throat.

This was it – the place where all my dreams would finally come together.

We bid a polite farewell to Mr Rossetti and then followed the butler inside the palazzo. He ushered us through a large, oval-shaped entrance with a speckled terrazzo floor and lined with Maiolican vases on marble pedestals. The Gianelli family had obviously retained their wealth over the past generations. As he showed us into the parlor, I noticed a sweet-faced, slender young woman with Titian hair sitting on a brocade settee; she seemed in deep conversation with another woman, older and heavier, dressed in a black habit.

The nun swung her glance toward us as we entered, and I stumbled slightly on the Persian carpet when I saw her identity: Sister Anna – the abbess of the Convent of San Giovanni.

I gasped. Of all the situations that I had imagined over the last day, this was certainly not one of them. After a few moments to compose myself, I moved forward again, striving to keep my emotions on a firm rein. The butler quietly stepped out and closed the doors behind him.

'*Buongiorno. Io sono Bianca.*' The young woman smiled and motioned for us to be seated across from her. 'I assume you are Signora Clairmont and Signor Trelawny.'

I nodded calmly, but my mind had begun to race with the various reasons for the nun's presence.

'*Questa è la Suora Anna—*'

'Yes, we are acquainted with the abbess,' Trelawny interjected with a touch of irony in his voice. 'The real question is how do you know her and, more importantly, why is she here today of all days?'

Bianca's face shadowed in puzzlement as she looked back and forth between the nun and us. 'Sister Anna is a longtime family friend . . . she saved my mother's life when she attended the convent school in Bagnacavallo all those years ago, and we have always kept in touch with her. She wrote to me several days ago about coming for a visit. It is just happenstance that she was still here when you called.'

'I hardly think so,' I muttered. 'The reason we asked to meet with you is that my daughter, Allegra, was also a pupil at the convent when the typhus epidemic struck; she, too, grew very ill, and I was told at the time that she died. But recently, I have come to believe that she did not succumb to the fever and may, in fact, have been smuggled out while she was still alive, and then hidden away ever since.'

'Is that even possible?' She raised her palms in a gesture of disbelief.

'Yes,' Trelawny said shortly. 'Did your mother ever mention a fellow pupil named Allegra Byron?'

'I . . . I do not think so. She rarely spoke of her days at the convent, except to praise Sister Anna, of course.'

The abbess said nothing, but her face paled.

'Are you certain, Signorina?' I pressed.

Weighing the question, she absently traced a pattern on the rich material of the settee. 'I do not recall her mentioning that name . . .'

A twinge of disappointment tugged at me. 'May we speak with her?'

Bianca pointed at a gilt-framed portrait of a lovely woman with large eyes and a generous mouth that hung on the wall. 'Sadly, she died from influenza five years ago. I thank God I had Sister Anna's support to help me through my grief. I do not think I could have survived without it.'

And yet we do survive . . .

'I am sorry that I cannot help you further,' Bianca said in a sad tone.

'But Sister Anna, or should I say, the *abbess*, can.' Trelawny's eyes narrowed. 'Surely, she did not travel all this way to stare at the Ligurian Sea.'

Folding her hands on her lap, the abbess stared down. 'Whatever I did, it was because I had no other choice. I thought if you believed that Allegra died, you might give up on your quest to find her, but I realized after your last visit that I had made a mistake and it would not take long for you to end up in Livorno. So I wrote to Bianca a few days ago and—'

'Did Allegra survive the typhus?' I blurted out. 'Will you please tell the truth, once and for all?'

'*Sì.*' She looked up, her eyes clear and direct. 'After Antonia's parents came for her, Tita showed up and took Allegra away while she was still alive; he and Lord Byron arranged to hide her away while she recovered.'

A flood of emotion washed over me, an odd combination of relief and pure rage.

'So Father Gianni *did* contact you a few weeks ago about Allegra?' Trelawny grated the query. 'You lied about that as well?'

'You must let me explain,' she began in a low, even tone. 'I grew up with Gianni and his brothers. They were quite poor, yet he and Gaetano rose above it; Stefano could not. He was the youngest, spoiled and selfish, wild at heart and willing to do anything for money. But Gianni and Gaetano thought they could control him, even when he became passionately involved

with the Carbonari.' She bit her lip. 'About that time, I joined
the Capuchin order as a postulant and was completely unaware
of what was occurring in Ravenna, until Lord Byron brought
his daughter to the convent, and I was placed in charge of her.
Gianni came to see me not long afterwards and said Allegra
was in great danger, and he suspected Stefano was somehow
involved. He made me promise not to betray his confidence
until he knew for certain—'

'Then Stefano appeared at the convent,' Trelawny added on
a grim note.

'Exactly.' The abbess visibly shuddered. 'It was frightening,
and after that we could not let Allegra out of our sight.'

'But why would he want to harm her?' I posed, my anger
dissipating slightly as I saw the anguish on her face.

She spread her hands in helpless appeal. 'Unfortunately,
Gianni never revealed Stefano's motivations, and I can only
assume it was fueled by hatred and resentment of Byron's
wealth. Not everyone in Ravenna supported Byron's role with
the Carbonari. After the *rivoluzione* fell apart, Stefano disappeared, but the danger had not ended. Typhus then struck the
convent, Allegra sickened, and I was afraid that she would
die. So, in the cover of night, Tita removed her from
Bagnacavallo. Only the old abbess and I knew she was taken
away, and they kept her location secret even from us as she
recuperated from her illness. Not knowing when or if Stefano
would return, Lord Byron made elaborate financial arrangements with Gianni to place Allegra in hiding – paid in cash,
gold, and other valuables – with him as the sole intermediary.
In gratitude for our assistance, Lord Byron donated a valuable
painting to the convent: the Madonna of Bagnacavallo, which
is an original work by Albrecht Dürer.'

Of course – the portrait in her office.

A priceless artifact.

Lowering her arms again, the abbess fell silent.

'Why did you and Father Gianni not tell me all of this?' I
asked, my ire stirring again. 'It would have prevented so much
hardship and tragedy.'

'He did not know Allegra was your daughter until you
confessed to him that day in his basilica. He was shocked.

Afterwards, he wrote to me, saying that he intended to tell you the truth since Stefano was long dead. But then Father Gianni was murdered, and I became fearful that the evil had not passed with him, so I kept silent.'

Trelawny glowered at her. 'What about Matteo?'

'I knew nothing about him, or whether he acted alone or not when he stabbed Gianni. I was devastated when my old friend was killed.'

Bianca stiffened as a touch of alarm lit her face. 'Does that mean this killer might have followed you here to Livorno?'

'No – Matteo is dead,' I hastened to assure her. 'And the *polizia* are investigating a criminal who might have been his accomplice.'

She did not look completely convinced.

'Believe me, it is true.' I turned back to the abbess. 'Do you know where Allegra is, or if she is still alive?'

A scuffle outside the door caught my attention, and the door swung open. Georgiana came rushing in and threw herself on my lap. In her wake, Paula and Raphael stumbled into the room with stiff, awkward steps.

Something was wrong.

'What are you doing here?' I took in their tense faces and bedraggled appearances as I gave Georgiana a reassuring hug. 'I expressly forbade you to come.'

Baldini slowly rounded the corner behind them, a pistol in his hand. 'We could not wait.'

Instantly, Trelawny jerked to his feet.

'Sit down.' Baldini leveled the gun at him, and Trelawny complied reluctantly.

'What is the meaning of this, Lieutenant?' I asked in dazed confusion. 'Did my niece persuade you to come here?'

Paula shook her head violently. 'No, *he* forced us to tell him where you had gone, then made us accompany him when he found out the Cades sketch was not at our apartment – I offered him your Byron/Shelley letters instead, but he would not accept them.' She collapsed in a chair, sweeping back her disheveled hair; Raphael stood next to her, a protective hand on her shoulder.

'I still do not understand.' Holding Georgiana even more

closely, I struggled to take in the lieutenant's sudden change of behavior. 'Why have you brought my family here?'

'He wanted "incentives" to make certain you agree to his demands,' Trelawny said, not taking his eyes off the lieutenant, 'and intends to harm them if you do not agree.'

'You must not do this,' the abbess warned Baldini, grasping her rosary. 'God is watching you, my son.'

Baldini gave a scoffing laugh. 'Do you believe your pathetic religion will sway me from my mission? I believe in nothing but myself.'

When he moved forward, Bianca reached for the servants' bell; Baldini swung the gun in her direction. 'I would not do that.'

She dropped her arm immediately.

'Everyone just stay still, and I will not hurt you.' Baldini waved the pistol back and forth like a talisman. 'I will forget about the sketch, but I want the rest of Allegra's *tesoro*.'

I stared at him in disbelief, my heart pounding. 'What treasure?'

He flashed a contemptuous look at me. 'You think everything that has happened has been over a piece of artwork and some letters from those worthless poets you so loved? Do not be foolish. There is much more at stake and always has been.'

A sudden realization clicked in my mind. 'You were in on the plot with Matteo?'

'I used him to achieve my own ends,' he said slowly, deliberately.

'But—'

'*Silenzio!* You still do not see the larger picture, Signora Clairmont. I will grant that you found pieces of the torn canvas from the past, but you are missing key sections – the ones that really matter. It goes back a long, long way, to when you were in Geneva during that summer of 1816. You did not fall down those stairs at Castle Chillon; you were pushed by Stefano Costa – di Breme's servant – because he wanted Byron to come to Italy and fight with the Carbonari. Having a mistress like you might have kept him from going. Of course, di Breme knew nothing about it, though he suspected you were with child; he had come only to talk with Byron about joining the Italian revolutionaries, and even that was clandestine.'

A secret mission. It did not surprise me since I had recently already suspected some of it. At least I now fully understood that Mary and Shelley had no knowledge of this plot.

'How did you learn all of this?' Trelawny said, his voice hard as stone.

'Please, let me finish.' Baldini swept his gaze indifferently across all of us, halting on me. 'You did not die, but Byron was too cautious to bring you and the unborn child with him. So he sent you to England, and he came to Italy to join the Carbonari. But the rebellion did not go well, and Stefano became more and more obsessed that Byron was not doing enough or committing enough of his vast financial resources. He tried to steal from Byron. He even schemed to assassinate him. Eventually, he attempted to kidnap Allegra to hold her ransom, but that failed as well.' His lips twisted in a cynical smile. 'His brothers, Gianni and Gaetano, tried to reason with him, but he would hear none of it. He knew Gianni later conspired to hide Byron's daughter and oversaw the wealth Byron had settled on her, but he refused to share the riches with Stefano. Why could he not secretly hand some of it over to his brother? But, no, Gianni would not hear of it.' He muttered a curse. 'When Byron later amassed a war chest to finance the Greek war, Stefano thought he would have another chance to steal some of Byron's riches, so he hired that fool Vitalis to sail aboard the *Hercules* to find a way to pilfer it, but he failed in the task because Gaetano found out and also booked passage on the ship to protect Byron. So, Stefano secretly traveled to Greece himself to give it one last try on the pretext of joining the revolution. All he wanted was a share of Byron's wealth, and he would not have given up; unfortunately, the English lord died before he could achieve his goal.'

'Who are you?' Paula spoke up in a shaky voice.

He paced slowly around the room, then stopped. 'I am Stefano Costa's son.'

The room turned deadly quiet.

'After Byron's death, my father had no desire to come home, so he stayed hidden in Greece until Gaetano stopped searching for him and, later, decided to live openly in a remote mountain village after the revolution was over. Eventually, he married a local girl who died giving birth to me.' A shadow passed over his face.

'What happened to Vitalis?' Trelawny queried.

A sly smile spread over Baldini's face. 'He was silenced forever.'

Dear God. Stefano had become a monster.

'As I grew to manhood, my father told me this story of being thwarted in his schemes many, many times, almost as if he wanted me to feel the pain with him. He became more and more despairing as time went by and, eventually, died a bitter, impoverished man. Once he had passed away, there was nothing for me there, so I moved to Florence, took a new identity, and bided my time – watching and waiting for Father Gianni to reveal something so that I might avenge my father by getting what he had always desired. I joined the police and stayed close to Gianni, knowing he still administered the small fortune Byron settled on his daughter; all I needed to find out was her whereabouts. It finally happened when I overheard you, Signora Clairmont, telling the priest about your daughter that day in the basilica. I would have wrung her location out of him, but Matteo killed him first over those stupid letters, which meant nothing to me. But, then, the Cades sketch appeared, which I arranged for Matteo to steal from you.' He paused. 'I trailed you to Ravenna with him to help him find a buyer for the drawing, and I had to make sure Gaetano could not talk once Trelawny contacted him—'

'You killed your own uncle?' I blurted out.

'Well, let us just say the shock of seeing me did the deed.'

The abbess crossed herself.

'I assume you are responsible for the *cinquedea* and all the violent acts that followed in Ravenna?' Trelawny posed with the sharp precision of a verbal knife. 'To stop us?'

'No.' He smiled. 'To drive you on to learn the truth about the signora's daughter.'

My stubbornness was our undoing.

Inhaling deeply, I began in a calm tone, 'I am sorry that Stefano led such a sad life, and that you did not have the love and kindness you deserved from him. I, too, had none of that because I never knew my own father. But please consider that what you seek does not belong to you.'

'It is recompense for what my father endured,' he retorted. 'I want everything left that Byron bequeathed to his daughter, and whatever he left to the convent to maintain the abbess's silence.'

She halted praying over the rosary beads. 'All we own is the Madonna of Bagnacavallo – the painting that hangs in my office – but, as I told Signora Clairmont, only Father Gianni knew how to access the money set aside for Allegra. I have no idea of where it is or even how much is left.'

'You lie.' Baldini's pleasant air dissipated as he aimed the pistol at her.

'Enough of this madness.' Trelawny stood, holding himself at full height, shoulders squared. 'Have not enough people suffered and died because of your father's greed? You have allowed his obsession to twist your own soul until you have become a mirror image of him . . . but you cannot shoot all of us with one pistol.'

Raphael moved quickly to position himself in front of Paula.

'All I need is one shot.' He swung the pistol in my direction, the barrel pointed at Georgiana.

I screamed and wrapped my arms around her for protection.

Trelawny and Raphael both threw themselves at him, and the gun went off – a piercing crack that reverberated through the room.

I froze, not sure if I had been wounded, but I felt no pain. Raising my head, it seemed like everyone was moving slowly . . . as if they had stepped into a place where time stilled to a crawl. Trelawny wrestled Baldini to the floor and Raphael grabbed his pistol while the lieutenant kept yelling *'Tesoro!'* again and again.

Then I spied a red stream of blood flowing down the front of the abbess's habit, and she tipped over to the side, her rosary falling from her fingers. *My God!*

I quickly handed Georgiana to Paula and knelt next to the nun, trying to staunch the wound with my handkerchief while holding her upright in the chair. She was bleeding profusely now. 'Call for a doctor – she is badly injured.'

Bianca rushed to the door at the moment it opened and Mr Rossetti appeared. 'I thought I would stop in and—' He broke off as he took in the scene of Baldini flailing on the floor under Trelawny's strong grip, and the wounded nun moaning in distress. He remained fixed for only a few seconds before dashing off for help.

'I . . . I must ask you again to forgive me, Signora Clairmont,' the abbess managed to gasp out. 'I have sinned against you and deserve to pay for it with my life; I can only hope that God will extend mercy to my soul.'

'Do not speak like that,' I said firmly. 'You are not going to die.'

She clutched at my arm. 'I truly have no idea where Allegra lives or if, indeed, she is still alive. Gianni was the only one who knew. The only thing he ever told me was that Allegra had little memory of her childhood before the fever but was happy in her life afterwards. *Perdonami.*' Her head rolled to the side as she lost consciousness.

As the abbess's words sank in, I faltered for an instant in maintaining the pressure against her wound.

My darling daughter was truly lost to me.

Father Gianni had taken the secret of Allegra's whereabouts to his grave . . . but at least I now knew she had not only survived but flourished.

Perhaps I could finally let go of her.

If today's events had taught me anything, it was to know when to release a hopeless dream before it became a tortured delusion.

Redoubling my efforts to keep the abbess alive, I refused to stop until the doctor had arrived and dressed her wound; he declared her injury was not fatal since the bullet had not punctured her heart. I was relieved, in spite of everything she had done. In her own way, she had loved Allegra.

Then the *polizia* came for Baldini who spat at us as he was taken away, and I thanked God that his murderous evil was finally out of our lives.

We were truly safe now.

Bianca ordered a herbal tea to calm our nerves, and we all sat quietly for an hour or so until Raphael eventually summoned the energy to escort Paula and Georgiana out; I embraced them all before they exited, promising that we would meet later this evening to celebrate the end of our long nightmare – and Paula revealed that Raphael had been promised the job of *tuttofare* at the Palazzo Cruciato. My heart sang with delight. I would mourn not finding Allegra later. But, first, we would give thanks that we were all safe and that, finally, Raphael and Paula could begin their life together as man and wife.

Yet Trelawny and I remained a little longer, not only for me to apologize one last time to our hostess for bringing such terror to her home, but to linger a few more moments with Bianca – my last contact to Allegra. I could not let go yet.

'I hope you will be able to find it in your heart to pardon us,' I began. 'We never meant to place you in harm's way.'

'It was not your fault, Signora,' she said generously. 'Had the roles been reversed, my own mother would have never rested until she found me.'

'*Grazie.*' I hesitated as Trelawny tried to draw me to the door. 'I must ask you one last time: are you absolutely certain that your mama never mentioned Allegra?'

'*Sì.*'

So it was truly over.

Sighing deeply, I took one last look at the painting of Bianca's mother. As I started to turn away, my glance fell upon a portrait cameo on the table beneath it. It featured the lovely face of a woman holding up a wildflower which partially obscured her features, but something about her eyes looked familiar. I picked it up to hold it closer, but still could not make out her features. 'Who is this?'

'Oh, that is my mother's cousin who lives a few miles away,' she said, taking it from me and kissing the image. 'She has always been a bit reclusive but is almost like a second mama to me. Her name is Alba.'

Trelawny and I exchanged glances.

The name I had chosen originally for Allegra – it meant 'sunrise.'

Perhaps the light had finally dawned after all.

Could it be?

TEN

'There be none of Beauty's daughters
With a magic like Thee . . .'

Byron, 'There Be None of Beauty's Daughters,' 1–2

Livorno, Italy
July 1873

I was almost too excited to speak as the carriage headed south of Livorno.

In less than an hour, I would know the answer to the question I had been seeking almost my entire life, and it would be near the Villa Valsovano where I had once stayed with Mary and Shelley. How fitting. I had spent Allegra's third birthday there without her because she was in Ravenna with Byron; I so wanted to see her, but he would not agree. Perhaps today would make up for that lost reunion.

'Have you recovered from the trauma yesterday?' Trelawny asked from his seat next to me. 'I probably should not have agreed to escort you on this trip after the horrid events at the Gianelli villa, but I never could resist your requests. At least our gathering last night with Paula and Raphael brought a slight sparkle back to your eyes'

'It was seeing the triumph of their love – and having my faith in Father Gianni's intentions somewhat restored.' I smiled. 'Even without all of that, though, nothing would have stopped me from this final trip.'

'I know.' He swung his gaze to the flat terrain dotted by cypress trees. 'Claire, I was waiting for the right time to tell you, and I suppose this is as good as any . . . Teresa Guiccioli's passing was in the newspaper this morning. She must have died the day after we left Ravenna.'

'So soon? I shall mourn her – truly.' Closing my eyes for a moment, I recalled her sweet face when we parted, appealing even in old age. 'I see why Byron loved her. It was because she wanted nothing from him, unlike the rest of us who basked in his fame and craved his regard. I desperately tried to make him the great romance of my life, my one and only true and great love, but that was not in his nature, was it?'

'No, but he loved you in his own way,' Trelawny said, turning back to me. 'Never doubt that.'

'At least we created a beautiful child out of our brief union.' I reached for my bag and pulled out the last letter that Pietro had written to Teresa. 'I, too, had something to share with you and wanted us to read it together.' I began to recite it aloud . . .

Missolonghi, Greece
April 1824

My dearest Teresa,
I am sorry that I have not written in many months. We have been in Greece since January, and this marshy, wretched swamp of a town has proven also to be a mire of political infighting.

After Byron's landing at Missolonghi with full military honors, much like his idol George Washington, I saw every citizen's countenance content and lit with hope, but it has turned to impatience. The Greek leaders look to Byron to take charge of the revolution, but they balk at following orders from an Englishman. So his every suggestion, every proposal is questioned by them.

Surprisingly, he is not wearied by these conflicts; he is energized by them. At least now they are listening to him.

I must say, Missolonghi is a peculiar place – the sea and sky meet in one blurry natural canvas of whiteness. No division. No lines. Just an endless, opaque landscape. Our house is on the lagoon, with men coming and going at all hours of the day and night as Byron is drawn into the endless tasks of planning military operations.
I want to see action.

Still, I do not regret committing myself to this honorable enterprise; we will prevail.

Lately, we have been subjected to the most vicious and brutal winter storms. The last one was particularly bad, and we all caught colds, including Byron, which caused us to be housebound. Days and days of cold rain followed; even when we were well again, we could not ride on the impassable roads. Fortunately, Byron was able to direct the troop actions through couriers, dividing the resources between Mavrocordato and Odysseus who are constantly vying with each other for Byron's support and money. They both want to stake their claim as to who will lead the country once it is free.

Byron does not trust either of them, but he knows how to play each one against the other, always moving toward the ultimate goal of a free Greece.

My only sadness is that Gaetano has left us to look for his absent brother. Before he departed, he assured me that I was more dear to him than his lost sibling. I shall content myself with that declaration.

But I will miss him.

19 April 1824

This next part of my letter will be painful, dear sister, so prepare yourself.

After the skies finally cleared with the arrival of spring, Byron had a breakthrough in his talks with the Greek leaders, and he took a long horseback ride along the coast but, later, became feverish. He improved, but then quickly worsened – often sounding delirious; I could not stay in his room because a flood of tears rushed into my eyes. I feared for him.

Dr Bruno eventually decided to bleed Byron, which caused him to grow even weaker.

Then, two days ago, a violent sirocco started to shake the house with hurricane-like winds, and Tita said nature had begun to weep.

I did not need to ask what he meant; I knew.

*Inside the house, it had turned calm, and Byron seemed
to know the end was near. We kept vigil around his bed
and, at one point, Byron took Tita's hand and exclaimed,*
'Oh questa e una bella scena.'
It was *beautiful – and terrible.*

*As the thunder roared, Byron took his last breath at
a quarter past six – and the world came to a stop. He
died in a strange land, and among strangers, but more
loved, more mourned, he could not have been.*

*He died a hero and his death will inspire all of Greece
to come together and eventually achieve victory.*

Your desolate brother,
Pietro

I set the letter down.

'I should have been there with him at the end, but I swear
by all that is holy, I could not make it through the flooded
roads from Patras. For two days, I waded waist-deep through
the mud to get to his sickbed, but it was too late.' Trelawny's
voice grew thick with emotion. 'I tried. By God, I tried.'

'Of course you did, and he undoubtedly knew it.' Carefully
refolding the letter, I slipped the sheaf inside Trelawny's
volume of Byron's verse, tucked away in the pages of his
poem 'The Dream.' Then, I set it on the seat between us with
a sense of finality. *No more living in the past.* 'He believed
and trusted in you enough to share the secret of Allegra's fate,
which speaks to his regard for your loyalty.'

He squeezed my hand. 'Thank you, Claire.'

'Perhaps the hour has come for us to finally lay him to rest,'
I said, entwining my fingers with Trelawny's much larger ones.
'We have lived with Byron's ghost long enough and, after everything that happened yesterday, all of our questions have finally
been answered. It is time to let him go. Little else remains.'

'Except one thing.'

'Yes – Allegra.'

As we stayed hand in hand, watching the gracefully rolling
landscape pass by, I suddenly felt the presence of Mary and
Shelley with us, almost as if they sat in the carriage, as they
had done so many times when we traveled through Italy

together, eager for adventures. *I am so sorry I ever mistrusted you, my dear ones. Our days together are among my most precious memories.*

'Do you feel them with us?' Trelawny whispered.

My mouth curved in sweet assent.

Scarcely a few minutes later, the carriage halted in front of a small, gemlike villa covered in ivy vines and wildflowers.

At first, I did not move as my feelings shifted so wildly between fear and bliss that I could barely breathe. *Could I take having my hopes dashed yet again?*

'Go on, Claire,' Trelawny urged. 'This is *your* moment of truth.'

I touched his cheek. 'Will you wait for me?'

'Always.'

The driver helped me out of the carriage, and I slowly walked up the crooked, stone path to the front door. In my mind's eye, I saw Byron standing there in the sunlight, his handsome face beaming in approval; then, as I blinked, his image gradually faded into only a silent echo of his presence.

Farewell, my love.

The door swung open, and a still-youthful woman with blue eyes and a dimple in her chin appeared in the archway. She wore a *cornetto* pendant at her throat.

Allegra.

AUTHOR'S NOTE

Claire Clairmont never accepted that Allegra died at the Convent of San Giovanni at Bagnacavallo in 1822. She lived out her final days, though, satisfied that she had moved heaven and earth to find her daughter. Claire passed away in her beloved city of Florence, Italy, before her eighty-first birthday on March 19, 1879, and is buried under the pavement of the arcades in the public Cemetery of Antella. Only a simple plaque notes her name and date of death.